Dear Diary

Dear Diary

Niko Michelle

www.urbanbooks.net

Urban Books, LLC
300 Farmingdale Road, NY-Route 109
Farmingdale, NY 11735

ISBN 13: 978-1-64556-525-3

First Mass Market Printing October 2023
First Trade Paperback Printing November 2022
Printed in the United States of America

10 9 8 7 6 5 4 3 2 1

Distributed by Kensington Publishing Corp.
Submit Orders to:
Customer Service
400 Hahn Road
Westminster, MD 21157-4627
Phone: 1-800-733-3000
Fax: 1-800-659-2436

Entry 1

Dear Diary:

I killed my husband.

There, I said it. Well, wrote it. Same thing. An admission was an admission. It would have never made a difference if I owned it or not. Negative perceptions of me had already been formed. I was automatically guilty the minute I was arrested. Once my mug shot flashed across the news, circulated on social media, and saturated every newspaper, I was considered a monster, and there was nothing I could do to change how people viewed me.

Mr. Porter, my prison counselor, thought differently. "If you want to begin the healing process, Eva, the first thing you need to do is offer a confession without adding a 'but' and without placing the blame on anyone else," he told me and then gifted me with a generic black-and-white composition book to record my thoughts. "Start with this. Let's call it a diary if that helps to make it fun."

"I don't know what I'm supposed to do with this. I'm too old to be writing in diaries," I said and slid the book back in his direction. Every diary that I had owned or ever laid eyes on was decorative and came with a lock and key. What he gave me was not equipped to protect my secrets. Invasion of privacy was part of the reason I was in this place. Not even the strongest diary could handle my private thoughts.

"I want you to own the reason you're here. Document every detail as best as you can remember. There may be something discoverable that can lead to your conviction being overturned. And if not, it may be therapeutic, and healing can begin." Mr. Porter tapped his pale knuckles twice against the brown circular table and made his exit. Every time he'd come around after that, he always inquired about my journaling progress. The pages were still as white as the two strands of hair determined to have a forever home atop his freckled bald head.

Mr. Porter didn't do anything wrong. He tried hard to counsel me. I didn't trust him in the beginning, though. To me, he was a waste of my lingering time. Another fake investor pretending to care. During our first meeting, I had already convinced myself he was just another creep sent to take advantage of me like the correctional officers. Some of us girls were their freaky sex slaves, and there was nothing we could do about it but bend over and take it in whatever hole they decided to enter. It was mainly the backside to ensure we didn't get pregnant. Mr. Porter presented nice, but why would he be any different from the guards or Coach Cain?

Outside of my family, Coach Cain was supposed to be my protector. I trusted my middle school track coach, who I looked up to. I trusted him to train me physically. I trusted him to prepare me for a great future. Coach Cain was supposed to help me, not help himself to me in a way. He had only inappropriately touched me, but that was still too much.

It started with, "Eva, your calf muscles are poppin'. I'm impressed. Keep up the good work." I never thought anything of it. Nothing more than a compliment from my mentor and coach.

"Thank you," I'd respond to every compliment, smile, and work harder. I lived for the positive press. Finally, someone who thought I did something right, and if my coach felt that way, I just knew other people would too once they saw my speed. In my mind, every news station would begin to report on me, and everyone would want a piece of the Eva action and see me as something other than weird.

Things changed a bit for me the day before my first official meet. "Yeah! That's what I'm talking about. That's how you run." Coach Cain snatched his plain black cap off his head and threw it to the ground, raving over my run time.

I slowed my pace and buckled over, trying to catch my breath. He came up behind me, still shouting, "That's how you do it!" Coach Cain then sprinted to the cooler, filled up a paper cup with Gatorade, and as I drank it, he smacked my butt. His hand lingered there a moment before he inhaled and added, "You definitely have a future in the Olympics."

When I frowned and gasped, he snatched his hand away. An awkwardness silenced the birds chirping and the passing sirens.

At first, I was surprised Coach Cain had touched me like that. He never had, nor had I seen him do it to anyone else. Although uncomfortable, I shrugged it off. That was sports for you. I'd seen it done a million times during NBA games. Coach Cain got too excited, anticipating my win and future, and reacted. No big deal. But then, he took it a step further.

With two fingers, he waved me over. "Eva, come on, let me stretch you."

"Yes, sir," I said and jogged over to accept another unordinary act. Coach Cain had never volunteered to physically assist me with stretching. Usually, he'd leave it up to me, and if he didn't like what he saw, he'd verbally correct me.

I lay and he hovered. Again, I didn't think anything of it. Coach Cain just wanted me to get the best out of my body.

"Oh, that feels good," I moaned as he added some of his weight to my thigh. Given that he munched on his nails like chicken wings, I was surprised to feel the light scratch he applied.

Coach Cain's moan matched mine when he replied, "You like that?" When he leaned in closer, the black shades that always hid his eyes fell from his face. For the first time, I saw his dark, round eyes up close. He had only coached me for a year, but even then, I had never seen him without those shades.

Sweat ran from his chocolate bald head and down the sides of his identical-colored face. It was hot, and I'd seen him sweat before, but never as much as he did at that moment. Liquid guilt, perhaps.

The way he rubbed me, I knew it wasn't right. There was so much I wanted to say. So many refusals, so many opportunities to tell him to stop, but I remained speechless. It wasn't that I wanted him to touch me. I was scared. I finally found something where people cheered for me, and I didn't want to do anything to ruin it. I just knew I was taking it wrong and that it would pass. But then, Coach Cain said, "The things I can do to you off this field . . ."

Thankfully, another student approached, causing Coach Cain to snatch his hand away from nearly fondling my vagina.

My first ever track meet and I missed it. The thrill of being the next Olympian was taken from me because a man I was supposed to trust tried to take advantage of me. I never told. Anytime someone asked why I no longer ran, I shrugged it off and said, "I couldn't be both an athlete and an honors student."

Coach Cain tried to talk to me one time after. He tried to say it was a misunderstanding. If that were the case, I wondered why he never tried to get me back on the field.

So because of the Coach Cains of the world, it took a while to connect to Mr. Porter. A person who was sent to really help me.

I pondered over the point of what good his help would do. I had already been sentenced to death, so in my opinion, it was a little too late for productive therapy sessions. But over time, he grew on me. His treatment of me never wavered. Always nice. Always encouraging. I was still human in his eyes, and I began to anticipate seeing him every week. And he never missed an appointment. Like clockwork, every Tuesday at 9:00 a.m., he'd strut into the dingy conference room wearing a pair of high-water slacks, a solid-color sweater, argyle trouser socks, and loafers and give me his undivided attention for an hour or so. He was that listening ear I needed until my death did us part. Our connection popped on like a switch and stayed.

"Guess what, Mr. Porter?" I said as if we were going to occupy what little time we had with a silly kiddie game.

He sat back in the wobbly chair, crossed his arms, and smiled, really in tune with hearing what I was about to say. "I can't wait to hear it," he replied.

"You're a good friend. Talking to you is like talking to my brother before he died. You get me just like he did. If I had a chance to do things over, I would want to have met you earlier in life. That way, I know I would have had a chance." I held my fist out for him to bump. He added an explosion sound and connected his cold knuckles to mine.

"Hmph," he said and sat quietly for a moment, either taking it all in or thinking of how to respond. "Well, I appreciate that, Eva. I have a confession of my own."

A broad smile parted my dry, chapped lips before it quickly faded. I was eager to hear his confession but also nervous. People tended to hurt me with their words of judgment regarding my uniqueness and with their unapproved sexual advances. I didn't think Mr. Porter would do anything like that, but there was still a possibility he would show me a different side of himself.

"I consider you a good friend as well. If I had a daughter, I would love for her to be as courageous as you," he said, taking my breath away. "You have been dealt a hand of life that many people wouldn't know how to play, yet you play it just hoping to fairly place. That is commendable."

A few tears fell. "Very few people have wanted me, Mr. Porter, so hearing you say that . . ." I paused, swiped the falling tears, collected myself, and continued. "I have a lot of respect for you."

In fact, I grew to love Mr. Porter and even yearned for his visits. Not in a romantic way. He wasn't my type. But then again, being locked away at a maximum-security women's correctional facility left little room to be picky. Even if I could, Mr. Porter wouldn't be it. He was a good listener, but he spent too much time fighting those two pieces of hair that always stood at attention close to his forehead. No matter how many attempts he made to smooth them down with the palms of his hands, they'd pop right back up. Plus, his pale skin sweated a lot. Maybe if he wore something other than sweaters during every season, his skin would be able to breathe. Sometimes, I would wonder if Mr. Porter hid his skin because he was afraid he'd catch something from within these walls. If he did feel that way, I couldn't say I blamed him.

One day, I became bold enough to ask. "Mr. Porter, I don't mean any offense, but I gotta ask.

Why are you always wearing sweaters? You know you live in Georgia, right?" I chuckled a little to lighten the intent of the question.

Mr. Porter rolled up his sleeves and revealed his arms, which were heavily covered in blemishes and scars. "For starters, I have a skin condition called lichen planus. It causes extreme itching. The long sleeves and thickness of the sweater help to keep the calamine lotion from seeping through and rubbing off on anything else."

I instantly felt bad. "I'm so sorry, Mr. Porter. I didn't mean to—"

"No worries, Eva," he said as he rolled one sleeve back down. "Everyone struggles with something. I'll let you in on another secret." He closed his eyes, rubbed his palms over those pesky, untrained double strands of hair, and made a startling confession. "You see these?" he said, pointing out old scars on his exposed arm. "I used to be a cutter."

I gasped and couldn't close my mouth.

"At first, I'd cut every time my parents drank and argued. Then when my skin condition flared up, I'd cut, hoping to cut out the itching."

Finally, I moved my mouth enough to ask, "Is that why you do this?" I waved my hand around and added, "Counseling?"

"I couldn't see myself doing anything else," Mr. Porter said.

No wonder we had an inexplicable connection. Not only did he suffer in silence like me, but when I first arrived in prison, I used to itch every day. I'd scratch my skin until it bled. I grew to enjoy picking at the scabs. It gave me something to do, so I didn't mind the sores. After a while, the itching stopped, and I got used to the disgust. Outside of the slop they fed us, the showers were the most disgusting part of being locked away. Often, the drains would cough up hairballs like a cat. I used to slip and slide running from it. I'd watched enough television to imagine it swallowing me whole or infecting me with some kind of flesh-eating fungus. As with everything else, I grew used to it. I'd pick up the ball of hair and stare at it, trying to see if I could identify the head it came from. Sometimes I could and sometimes I couldn't. And then there were times when I would tuck the hair underneath my armpit and sneak it back to my cell. It allowed me to feel the closeness of another person outside of Mr. Porter and, unfortunately, the guards.

Prison was home, and I had to make the best of the situation until the day I died.

Death. I couldn't wait. If the afterlife was anything like what I read about, I was ready to experience it. No sickness, no poverty, and no prison. And I'd be reunited with my loved ones. I'd miss Mr. Porter and the feeling that tickled my stomach every time he came around. I wasn't physically attracted to him, but his soul fed mine. He understood me and my issues. I guessed he also reminded me of my husband and the level of patience and understanding he had with me and what I dealt with.

Being behind bars with women who had been through hell and back and had been treated like trashy blow-up dolls, it was refreshing to have a conversation with a person who didn't expect anything in return and who could hold a serious discussion, especially on topics that never piqued my interest before.

"Eva, have you been following the presidential election?" Mr. Porter once asked.

I side-eyed him. "Mr. Porter, you see where I am and where I will forever be. You know I can't vote."

"So? That doesn't mean you can't keep up," he retorted. "You can still follow along and fight."

I shook my head. "It's pointless. I deserve what I have coming to me," I said whether I believed it or not.

He crossed one leg over the other and thought for a moment. "Have you ever had an interest in politics and how lawmakers are shaping our country? Especially with regard to the mental health population?"

I shrugged. "Honestly, Mr. Porter, I haven't given politics much thought."

"Why not?" he asked. "I mean, it does apply to you and what you're going through. Politicians who have no clue about mental health actually pass laws that impact individuals with a diagnosis. Isn't that scary? Doesn't that make you want to do something about it?"

I lowered my eyes and made circles against the table with my index finger. I felt kind of embarrassed that I had no clue about how laws impacted my health and that I didn't care to do anything about it to help myself or anyone else. "I hear you. I don't really know. After being here, not much scares me anymore."

"Don't just hear me with your ears. Also hear me with your mind," he added. "You still have time to change your circumstances. The president has the ability to pardon you, Eva. You can still fight this."

Mr. Porter had become so passionate about me and my fate, but I, on the other hand, was over it and didn't care what happened. I sat quietly, taking in his thoughts.

"Let me ask you this," he said and hit me with another question I'd never given much thought to. "You have never been treated fairly, so what are you going to do about it?"

I shook my head and reminded him of what I was convinced of. "It won't matter, Mr. Porter."

He heavily sighed. "Think of other people like you who don't have an advocate or a voice. During your free hour, visit the library, read up on civics. You may be in prison, but your mind is still free," he said and rose from his seat, ending our session early. He seemed frustrated with my lack of enthusiasm for fighting for myself against lawmakers.

I didn't want Mr. Porter to consider me a lost cause and stop coming around, so I told him, "I will look into it." I thought he knew I wouldn't. Out of respect for him and our developing friendship, I did start dabbling, though. At least I'd give him something.

However, confessing to my husband's murder didn't do any good. Nothing changed. Not one fairy-tale character appeared before me, waving a magic wand. Where was the fairy dust from the movies, the kind that dramatically floated about until it landed and caused an instant change in circumstances? I remained housed in the same eighty-five-square-foot humdrum cell, awaiting execution.

Honestly, I couldn't fully process how I felt about what happened. Sometimes a tiny hint of remorse crept in, but I'd quickly rationalize and replace the guilt with contentment. I was already rotting behind these walls, so there was no sense in adding more hopelessness to an already-unpleasant situation by reliving it through writing stupid journal entries. But because I had developed a tremendous amount of respect for my counselor,

I did it, not necessarily believing anything would change or that I would heal as he thought.

What was there to heal? What was there to wallow in other than losing my identity? I was no longer Eva Moss, or Eva Moss-Sanders if the short amount of time I was married was counted. Nor was I the fresh-faced, brown-skinned girl with the long, curly sandy brown hair who just wanted to live an ordinary life while battling an unaccepted illness. My identity had been reduced to inmate number 317706, the crazy murderer with the now-matted hair, acne, and bags under my eyes.

The voice in my head was why he died, not because of me. There were times when I couldn't distinguish between reality and imagination, so there was no way I could be solely responsible for such a heinous crime. Besides, my husband should have assumed responsibility for what happened to him. He had gotten a glimpse into who I was before he proposed to me.

Entry 2

Dear Diary:

I had known Myles Sanders for years. Not only did we attend the same schools, but he and my brother, Michael, were best friends. Despite repeated rejections, Myles aggressively pursued me, always inviting me out, always trying to buy me something from Mrs. Alexander, the neighborhood candy lady, and always complimenting me.

"Hey, beautiful," he'd say and hand me a pack of strawberry Twizzlers or sunflower seeds. And then sometimes it was, "You look pretty today," and he'd present me with a bag of gummy worms. Even, "I like your shoes." There was nothing spectacular about my shoes. Basic sandals or no-name colorful sneakers were my thing. Of course, I took the candy. I appreciated the snacks more than the attention or the crush.

Sometimes I thought Myles only came over as often as he did to see me and not Michael. I was convinced of that one Valentine's Day.

There was a knock at the door, and when I opened it, it was Myles, standing there cheesing, wearing a suit covered in flamingos.

"What in the world do you have on?" I asked, laughing hysterically.

"Where's Mike?" Myles asked.

I frowned and pursed my lips before I spoke. "You know better than to call him that, and you also know he hasn't made it home yet," I said. My mother always taught us to make people respect us by putting some respect on our names. There were no shortcuts. We were to answer only to the names she and my dad gave us.

"My bad," Myles said. "Is *Michael* home?"

"And again, you know he's not." Those boys talked every day. Myles knew exactly what time Michael would be home.

"Well, can I wait for him?" Myles asked.

My mother did not play that. No boys or girls in the house when she was not home. She made an exception for Myles only when Michael was home. "You know the rules," I reminded him.

"Can you bend them for me since it's love day?" Myles asked and pulled a rose and a tiny box of candy from behind his back.

I laughed harder. "I knew you loved my brother, but I didn't know you *loved* my brother," I joked.

Myles smacked his teeth. "Quit playing, Eva. This is for you."

"Why?" I asked with an ounce of attitude and confusion mixed.

"Is it not obvious?"

I shook my head and tried to close the door, but Myles stopped it with his foot.

"I like you, Eva. I was hoping we could hang out today, but I'll try again later. Tell Michael I stopped by." Myles laid the rose and candy in front of the door and walked away.

At first, I felt bad because it seemed as if I had hurt his feelings, but then taking in that flamingo suit again left me howling once more. Even though I let Myles down, he didn't stop. On Saint Patrick's Day, he pulled a similar stunt.

"Eva."

I heard my name and felt a tap on my shoulder. I rolled my eyes, seeing Myles standing near my locker with the same silly grin from Valentine's Day and wearing a green T-shirt that read, "The Luck of the Irish."

"Will you be my lucky charm?" he asked and presented me with a white rose and greeting card.

Other students stopped and admired his efforts, and because of that, I didn't embarrass him. "Thank you, Myles." I took the rose, never acknowledging his question, without him knowing that I was fuming on the inside.

Someone just had to say something smart. "Of all the girls, he chose the weird one."

I overlooked that comment as I did with every rude comment I heard about my personality.

Myles meant well, but I just wasn't into him. Like Mr. Porter, he was not my type. I didn't even know what my type was. But growing up, listening to the adults speak, I understood that a certain feeling would let me know when I was interested in a boy. Myles was not it. He didn't give me the butterflies or the giddy chuckles, nor did I blush when he came around.

He was too much of a goofball. Plus, he wore the craziest shirts, mainly with Hot Wheels flamed designs and animals. It was like the boy shopped at Toys "R" Us.

Once he transitioned from the awkward boy going through his puberty stage into a budding adult, he wasn't half bad. The nasty pustule acne eventually faded, revealing some of the most beautiful dark skin. The development of facial hair that lined his top lip and dangled from his chin made him look more mature. His voice went from a high-pitched whine to that of a baritone singer.

I still didn't like him, though. Plus, dodging his advances was the only way I could protect him. There was something wrong with me, but I didn't fully understand what at the time. Other than my brother, my mother was the only person who knew all wasn't well within me.

My mother believed in healing through faith. In her world, fasting, studying God's Word, and prayer would have eventually made my unique behavior disappear. She always said, "Eva, the Lord will work this out. Have patience and trust Him."

Then she'd recite a scripture and make me repeat it. "'Heal me, O Lord, and I will be healed: save me, and I will be saved, for you are the one I praise.'" We'd say that several times in one sitting, and when we weren't saying it, my mother found ways to remind me of it. Index cards were plastered throughout my path: stuck to the refrigerator, taped to my bedroom mirror, and a few times tucked in my lunch bag.

I tried, but it seemed to take forever. As much as my mother stayed on her knees—fingers intertwined, eyes closed, and mumbling—she had to have received an answer to her prayers sooner than when she reacted. I believed the answer to her prayers was for her to seek professional help for me. After all, that's why professionals were placed on earth with specific gifts.

I was confident my mother ignored the solution. Her reluctance to take me in for an actual diagnosis made me question if she relied on faith or if she was embarrassed by me or in denial. Her methods to fix me didn't work. However, my brother's presence had a calming effect on me. Most nights,

I would lie across his bed, watching him watch his muscles bulge as he stood in front of the full-length mirror, lifting forty-pound dumbbells. Three veins protruded at different angles from both of his sculpted biceps, and his abs counted two more than the standard six-pack. I'd fall asleep in his room, listening to what he called "Bedtime Stories by Michael."

"You wanna know something, Eva?" Michael asked.

I groaned, knowing the next thing that exited his mouth would be some foolery. And I was right.

"Other than going into the NFL, I think it's meant for me to have a compound full of women." The left weight thumped the floor when he dropped it against the carpet to flex. "All this can't be spared for just one woman."

Michael's foolishness would usually put me right to sleep.

It was the same routine for us the night he died. While he waited for Myles to pick him up for their senior party, he shared with me the corny pickup lines he planned to use to get girls.

"Check this out," he said and rubbed his hands together like he knew he'd be irresistible. "Your daddy must be a drug dealer, 'cause you're dope."

I returned a blank expression.

"Okay, how about this one?" he asked. "You must be a beaver, 'cause damn!"

The deep dimples that accompanied his smile made it impossible for me to tell him how many girls he'd run off if he said those things. But then again, he was a star football player with a bright future, and the girls were always after him. With an ego that was already too far gone, there was nothing I could do to save him.

Instead, I laughed. "See you when you get back. I can't wait to hear how those lines work out for you."

Michael never returned.

Many blamed Myles for my brother's death, including me. Myles was the drunk driver who ran the red light. He survived. Michael was sober and succumbed to the injuries he sustained in the accident.

Funny how it always worked out that way. The innocent expired while the offender got a second chance at life. Well, every offender except for me.

Entry 3

Dear Diary:

Years have passed since my brother's death, but I still remember it like it happened yesterday.

There was a forceful knock at the door. I just knew it was Michael, who often forgot his key.

"I shouldn't let you in," I yelled through the thick, wooden door as I unlocked the deadbolt. I swung the front door open and channeled my mother by resting one hand on my hip, ready to demand an explanation for why he missed curfew and, once again, didn't have his key.

Instead, it was the cops, two of them, looking for my mother. One was tall, skinny, and black, and the other was a short, stocky Hispanic officer. They both removed their hats and placed them against their chests. Only one spoke. "Good evening," the black officer said before introducing himself and his partner. "We are looking for Annie Mae Moss."

At first, I thought they were coming to take my mother to jail. I wouldn't let them. Besides, what could she have done to warrant a visit from the cops? All the lady did was work as a church secretary at the same church she spent more time at than she did at home. And on some days, she cleaned fancy office buildings for extra money. She'd come home late at night, kick the shoes off her swollen feet, and go straight to her Bible. She had no time to do anything wrong.

I was only around 16 at the time, but anything they needed to say to my mother could be said to me. "I'm Eva Moss, her daughter. Is there something I can help you with?"

The same officer spoke again. "We are here in regard to Michael Moss. Is your mother available?"

I would definitely protect him. If my mother found out about the police showing up at her door at nearly one in the morning, let's just say he'd be safer with them.

"I'm sorry, Officers. She is not available. But I can help you. Is my brother in trouble?"

"If you don't mind, we need to speak with your mother. It's critical."

Critical? That word concerned me. "Wait here," I nervously replied to the taller officer who'd done all the communicating.

When my mother finally shuffled her way to the door, I stood behind her to listen. I assumed there was a fight at the party and Michael was arrested. Or they were bringing him home for whatever reason. Never in a million years did I think I would hear death associated with Michael.

The black officer cleared his throat and hesitantly dropped the news. "I am sorry, ma'am, but Michael was killed in a car accident tonight."

My mother screamed out in agony. The wail that projected from her lungs matched the sound of the screeching car tires that had slammed on the brakes to avoid colliding with the police cruiser that took up most of the tiny street. I used my fingers to barricade my ears from the loud, painful cries.

"No, no. Please, Officers. I'm begging you." No matter how much my mother pleaded, the reason for the officers' visit didn't change. Tears stained her nightgown. "He's my only son." She cried harder and continued to mumble as she collapsed and squirmed around the floor like a fish out of water. The pink sponge rollers that were once neatly clipped to her hair were sprawled across the floor. The ones that held on for dear life dangled when the officers helped her to her feet.

"Is there anyone we can call for you?" the officer who had been silent asked.

My mother didn't answer. She only hid her eyes behind her palms and shook her head in disbelief.

The officer directed his attention to me. "Ma'am, is there a nearby relative we can call to come over?"

The view from my eyes was blank. I remained speechless and in shock.

He tried my mother again. "We'd be glad to call someone for you. Or if you need a ride somewhere . . ." His voice trailed off. His eyes were glossy, like he wanted to cry right along with my mother.

After multiple attempts to answer through hysteria, hoarseness laced my mother's words when she finally spoke. "My brother, Bobby. He'll come over. Robert Moss. I can get the phone." She tried to stand but was too weak and slumped back into the chair.

"Can you get your mother a glass of water?" the Hispanic officer asked.

I heard him, but I couldn't move. He found his way to the kitchen and came back with two glasses, one for my mother and one for me.

"Here you go, young lady." He held out the glass he had poured for me, but I didn't take it. "I'll put it here in case," he said, placing the glass on the coffee table.

"Ma'am," he said and handed my mother her glass. Unlike me, she accepted it. Her hands trembled as she downed the liquid in seconds.

I knew people's perception of police officers, and I wished they could have met the officers who assisted us, specifically the Hispanic one. He didn't know us, but it was like he hurt too.

"Is it okay that I dial your brother's number?" he asked.

"I can do it." My mother had finally calmed down enough to dial Uncle Bobby's number. When he answered, she screamed at the top of her lungs and couldn't get the words out.

The black officer took the phone and delivered the news. Twice I had to hear it.

Within minutes, Uncle Bobby came rushing over, and later in the day, so did a bunch of other people. Some I knew and some I didn't. Because I stayed in the same spot near the front door even after the officers left, I saw everything—every face, every tear, every balled-up tissue, every pan of chicken, every dry-looking pound cake, every pan of green beans—and I heard everything everyone said to and about me.

"Sorry for your loss," a somber-looking older neighbor with a massive run in her pantyhose expressed.

What loss? It was only a matter of time before Michael would appear alongside Ashton Kutcher and the *Punk'd* camera crew to confirm what I had convinced myself of. Michael was not dead. Even if that show didn't air anymore, they were going to make an exception for me. I just had to wait.

Every time someone went in and out the door, the cold breeze chilled me even more. I was wet, but I still couldn't move.

Soon, I heard, "Oh, Lord. What is that awful smell?"

The trickles of pee that ran down my leg had started to smell. The longer it stayed against my skin and in my clothes, the more potent it became. I could smell it too. It didn't bother me as much as it did everyone else. I was numb, like I had been injected with Novocain.

"Come on, dear," Aunt Clara whispered and lightly tugged at my arm. "Let's get you cleaned up." Clara was Uncle Bobby's wife and the sweetest woman I had ever met. With her sheer persistence, I wound up allowing her to run me a bath.

I soaked in the frigid water as if it were still warm and steamy. I didn't know how much time had passed, but when Clara came back to check on me, her tears mixed in with my bathwater. "You're shivering." She tested the water. "This water is freezing," she said through sobs. "I'm so sorry, dear. I didn't mean to forget about you. There's so much going on out there." When she realized that she had broken down, she apologized some more. "I'm sorry. I'm sorry. I'm supposed to be strong."

I could have said something to comfort her, at least let her know that it was okay, but I didn't.

Clara added more hot water and didn't flinch as she lathered up the washcloth and gently washed me like she was cleaning off a newborn baby. I didn't flinch either at the thought of someone see-ing me naked. She struggled, huffed, and puffed as she wiggled a pair of sweats over my thighs. She effortlessly fastened my bra, and after she rolled deodorant under my arms and brushed my hair, she guided me into the kitchen with everyone else.

"Who has the body?" an older relative asked.

"Williams," my mother said through sobs. "I never imagined I'd be planning a funeral for my child. God help me," my mother cried out.

Clara was right there to console her. In fact, Clara tried consoling everyone.

That same older relative fired off another question. "What day you looking to have the services, Annie?"

My mother was too choked up to answer, so Clara answered for her. "Hopefully Saturday, but we will see what the funeral home says."

And again, another question. "Michael have life insurance, or we passing the plate?"

I wanted so bad to tell her to shut up, but instead, I rolled my eyes in disgust.

"This is what we will do," Clara said. "The appointment to set arrangements is tomorrow. Once we get all that set, we will give you all the information you need. No need to collect any money for burial. Annie had the kids' affairs in order. Thank you, though." I loved how Clara pleasantly shut the disrespect down.

I was certain someone would go behind my mother's back and pass the plate, claiming Michael didn't have insurance, and pocket that change. There was one in every family.

After listening to conversations and potential funeral arrangements, and ignoring every question and comment directed toward me, I couldn't take anymore. I found myself waiting at the front door for Michael and once again soiling my clothes. This time, there was a puddle.

"Someone, please get this girl some Depends." I heard my cousin's attempt at a whisper on his way out the door. He was in his fifties and way too old to make snide remarks under his breath, especially about a child who was clearly going through something.

Clara heard him too. She ushered me away from the door and back to the bathroom, where she wiped me down again, dressed me in PJs, and sent me off to bed.

I didn't sleep a wink. I lay there still waiting for Michael. I counted sheep and waited. "One, two, three, four, five." Nothing. I was still wide awake, so I decided to name the sheep. "Sheep number one I'll name Michael. Sheep two, Clara." I paused and gave up once I realized how stupid that was.

I tried playing a game. For every footstep and noise I heard near my bedroom door, I tried to match it to the person. One time, I thought I heard my brother laugh. I jumped up and blew through the door like a storm.

"Michael!" I yelled as I rounded the corner. That had been the first and only word I had spoken to where anyone could hear me since the officers showed up. It wasn't that I intended to take a vow of silence, but I just didn't have anything to say to anyone outside of my best friend, who also happened to be my brother.

It was a false alarm. Michael still hadn't made it back.

"Michael's not coming back."

I turned toward my mother's whisper. She sat in a chair in the corner of the kitchen in the dark. She'd finally taken the rollers out, but even her hair's silhouette was a mess.

"Just be patient," I advised her and made my way back near the front door, where I patiently waited. Instead of ushering me away, Clara sat with me. She made small talk, introducing me to the different people she had encountered in life. That woman had a story for everything.

"I know how you feel, Eva. To be in shock. That shock is something. When my mother passed, boy, did that do something to me. Hmm, hmm, hmm. That was tough, and Michael's death will be tough. But it will get easier. One day at a time."

I turned to her and smiled. "Michael's not dead. He'll be back as soon as the party is over."

Clara didn't argue with me or try to persuade me otherwise.

I wished what I had said was true. Six days of waiting, and still no Michael. It wasn't until the

seventh day when I saw my brother lying in the
casket that I realized it was real. He looked as if he
were sleeping, but plastic. He was dressed in a suit
like he was going to an important job interview,
and a football rested near his head. Even still, for
a second, I believed he would jump up and give us
all a heart attack. Maybe even say his usual, "Go
long," and then throw the football to the back of
the church.

Even reading the words in his obituary, it still
didn't click. Clara and her creativity thought it
would be a good idea to have the obituary written
in first person as if the words were Michael's final
goodbye to everyone.

*On May 15, 2016, heaven needed a football
player, and they chose me, Michael Ronald
Moss, one of the fastest running backs with
Morrison High School.*

*I was born in Missionville, Georgia, on
March 22, 1998, to Annie Mae Moss and
the late Ronald Michael Moss. I'd like to
believe that instead of a wail to announce
my arrival, I roared, "Go long!"*

*I accomplished a lot during my short
time on earth. Not only was I an athlete
who led the county in rushing yards, but I
was preparing to graduate with a 3.6 GPA.
Everyone who knew me knew that I had*

dreams of gathering with my family on draft day and hearing my name called to join the Atlanta Falcons. My name was called for a bigger, better team, and I can't wait to play.

To my beloved mother, Annie Mae Moss, thank you for your unparalleled love. Keep praising the Lord, for I have joined His team. To my sister and bestie, Eva Moss, thank you for loving me unconditionally. It was a pleasure serving as your big brother. To all my aunts, uncles, cousins, and friends, jump on the Falcons bandwagon and keep an extra eye out for my girls.

If you shed a tear, allow it to be a tear of joy for the smiles I put on your faces, and not from sadness. God knew best. I will always be around. Just listen for what you think is thunder. It may very well be me scoring a touchdown.

It wasn't until the funeral director covered Michael's face, shut the casket light off, and closed the lid, that I mourned for the first time. My cries were similar to my mother's the night we found out he had been killed.

The funeral was the only day I cried. Each day that passed from there, my state worsened. I barely ate or slept. And that bathroom thing kept happening outside of the bathroom. My mattress looked like the place for potty training toddlers. Now it was my mother who had to drag me to the shower to clean me off multiple times a day.

So much for the spiritual beliefs that she believed would heal me. She'd finally had enough and had me committed.

Entry 4

Dear Diary:

I followed the yellow exit arrows, high-fived a passing orderly, and excitedly skipped around the corner.

"Where's my mom?" I asked Uncle Bobby and Clara as soon as I rounded the corridor and noticed them instead of my mother. My eyes darted around, searching, thinking she was within proximity.

Clara feigned a smile. "It's just us," she said, fanning her hand between herself and my uncle.

I was a little disappointed that my mother hadn't come. I couldn't wait to hug her. Usually, I hated the lingering scent of White Diamonds on my clothes, but I missed her. "Why didn't she come?" I asked, still looking around as if she were going to pop up from behind the desk or a wall.

Neither of them said anything. Uncle Bobby removed the beige Kangol cap that he wore every time he left the house. His face deepened with somberness. Clara pulled me into her flat chest and sniffled.

Because the two of them were quiet, so was I. Plus, they had made my release so weird that I wasn't sure I wanted to talk. It was *one* breakdown, and since I had started on an antidepressant, everything was going to be okay. They'd see my progress, and so would my mother.

In my ever-hopeful, daydreaming mind, I imagined that my mother stayed home to entertain the guests for my surprise welcome home party. A cheesy grin swallowed my eyes as I visualized walking into a roomful of loved ones with a large WELCOME HOME sign, balloons, and some good barbecue. We'd laugh and do the Electric Slide and play checkers and *Pictionary*. Michael would be there. Maybe. I hoped. At least in spirit. Even if he weren't, I'd try to be okay and enjoy all the love surrounding me.

As I inhaled the fresh air, I instantly became talkative and giddy, anticipating my freedom and party. "I can't wait to see my mom. I'd bet all the money in my piggy bank that she's up to something." If I were wrong, they wouldn't get much. From what I was told, that piggy bank was a baby shower gift from a family member, and my dad would add change to it every week. When he passed, my mother didn't carry on the tradition. I'd never thought much about cracking it open, but I would for a hint.

Again, they were both quiet.

I kept going. "It wasn't too bad in there," I said and tossed a final glance in the direction of the building. "The food was below average, but the workers seemed to really care about me."

"Oh, dear, that's really nice," Clara said and caught a falling tear with her knuckle.

"Are you okay?" I asked. "I'm better," I tried convincing her so she'd cheer up.

She pursed her lips, then tightly closed her eyes. "We will talk in the car."

I smiled thinking of how hard she was putting on to keep my party a secret.

Once inside the car, Clara climbed into the back seat with me. "Eva, there's no easy way to say this," she said and handed me an envelope that had already been opened. It was small and square like my mother used when mailing cards.

The front of the envelope was addressed to "The Family." Inside was a note that read:

> *To my dearest family,*
> *Do not mourn for me, for I will be at peace while in eternal rest serving God. He is a forgiving God, and I have prayed and asked for forgiveness from my family as well. I have decided to leave this earth. Losing both of my children has been the hardest thing to deal with. What good am I as a mother without them? To whoever takes on the*

*responsibility of raising Eva, please treat
her with care. She is a unique child, different
from what you may be used to. Please do not
be upset, for we will meet again.*

   Love,

   Annie Mae

Through a suicide note that I wished I had never
been privy to, I learned that I wouldn't have my
mother to go home to. All the misery she went
through with Michael's death and my insanity
proved to be too much for her.

Another loss.

Another funeral.

Another period of numbness.

The specifics of what happened were offered to
me, but I refused to hear them. Why would anyone
want to subject a 16-year-old child to such details
anyway?

Unfortunately, my refusals didn't block the un-
wanted details. I indirectly caught bits and pieces.
The adults would converse about my mother's
passing while sitting around the table or outside
sharing a smoke. They would fall silent when they
noticed I was nearby. By that time, it was too late. I
had heard more than I wanted.

It wasn't just the adults. The kids who were
always in grown folks' business decided to share
what they had heard with me. My head often

throbbed over the different versions of the story. It seemed like everyone added extra details to make it their own masterpiece. Each time, the story grew more ridiculous than the story before.

"I heard Annie hanged herself because of that crazy child," one of my mother's first cousins said. That crazy child would be me, and I could hear. That version of the story was probably the most accurate of them all. I believed that had I not added to what my mother was dealing with, she wouldn't have ended her life.

Then there was, "I heard Annie Mae was involved in a love triangle with the pastor, and when his wife found out, he ended things. She was so depressed that she killed herself."

"I heard that too," Aunt Nora's friend commented as if she belonged. "But instead of her killing herself, the wife did it and made it look like a suicide."

I couldn't stand that lady. She always clutched her purse and turned her nose up at me. I may have been a little off mentally, but I was no thief. I never understood why she came around if my presence made her so uncomfortable. Probably for the freebies. Moocher. She was always the first one in the dinner line, piling food on her plate like it would be the last meal she ate. She was also the last one in the dinner line, packing up to-go plates, carrying out bags of sodas, asking for this and that.

Plus, she wore the ugliest plum-colored lipstick. Well, her teeth wore most of it. So much for her "friends," because they never told her. They just let her walk around looking a mess.

"What if that crazy girl did it?" Uncle Buster suggested. Impossible. I was institutionalized at the time.

"Oh, well, ain't that a plot twist," Aunt Nora added, chuckling and high-fiving her friend. I had lost my mother, brother, and home. Nothing was funny.

I never liked my great-aunt either. Nora always sat around gossiping about others as if the rumor mill didn't run full-time articles on her and her behavior. I always said that when I became an adult and couldn't be punished, I would remind her of her character flaws in front of others to see how she liked it. Aunt Nora stopped coming around as much, and when she did, I didn't have enough courage to be disrespectful, not even to the other conspiracy theorists. I just let their thoughts run wild.

At least the kids were mild. "I heard your mama died by herself," one of my smaller cousins stated. It was hard to feel anger when looking at her snaggletooth and innocence. She only repeated what she had heard.

I never told anyone about the comments. Times were already tough for me, and I didn't want to create unnecessary drama. Uncle Bobby and Clara did me a favor by taking me in, especially since every family member objected. I heard those conversations too.

They had sat around, trying to decide who'd become my new guardian.

"Girls like her need to be in a group home," Aunt Nora said.

Uncle Buster always fed off of Nora's shade, so of course, he had something to say. "They can't just keep her locked up?" he asked. I wanted so bad to remind him that I wasn't a zoo animal, but I was sure it wouldn't have done any good.

"Hell, if Annie left behind a life insurance policy or if she gets state benefits, I'll take her," Aunt Nora's friend said. "I can use some good ol' food stamps. But I'm adding a chain and lock on my bedroom door." She laughed hysterically.

"You all should be ashamed of yourselves," Clara said, coming to my defense. "She's a child, and she didn't ask for any of this to happen to her."

"Well, you and Bobby take her," Uncle Buster growled.

"Oh, we most certainly will," Clara snapped.

And they did, which I was grateful for. To be uprooted from the comfort of my home and forced to make a life with my aunt and uncle did nothing to cure the feelings of hopelessness. Neither did the antidepressant.

Entry 5

Dear Diary:

Living with Uncle Bobby, Clara, and their twin sons was okay. Their presence didn't fill the void of my mother and brother, but at least I wasn't alone, in foster care, or dumped on a relative who was only in it for the money.

My new family was loving. Even with the backlash they endured for taking in a girl like me, their commitment to caring for me never wavered. The backlash was partly their fault, though. The two of them gossiped like an entertainment blog. Their chatter was like a lighter, and once the lighter lit the brush known as my mental illness, the fire spread and scorched relationships. I believed it was unintentional, but a muzzle wouldn't have hurt. Uncle Bobby and Clara were old, confused, and trying to process their new life, as I was. Talking was probably therapeutic for them. I wished they would have chosen better people to vent to.

Or maybe I should have spoken up. Perhaps then the comments would've stopped. Instead, every time I needed a mental health boost, Uncle Bobby and Clara told the entire family about my recurring hospital stints. It was hard to escape the judgment because Uncle Bobby and Clara's house was the place for Sunday dinners and family gatherings.

"Excuse me," I interrupted the conversation taking place.

Several scowls burned my flesh.

"Yes, dear?" Clara said.

"May I walk the kids to Ms. Alexander's?"

Clara smiled. "Sure. Do you need any money?"

"No, ma'am. I still have the twenty you gave me last week." While my mother couldn't always afford to provide Michael and me with pocket change, Clara made sure I never went without. I was used to going without, so I hardly spent any of what she gave me.

"Will you be able to handle all those kids, or do you need me to walk with you? I don't mind," Clara said. "Us old folks are just sitting around here talking off this food. And I ate two slices of cake, so I can stand to walk some of it off."

"I got it," I confidently replied. I walked the twins to the store all the time. Three more kids wouldn't hurt. Besides, I loved being able to show off how responsible I was.

The kids were excited. They'd thrown their jackets on and jumped around like they had already swallowed a bunch of sugar.

"Um, Gerald can't go." Clara's sister pulled her
6-year-old grandson into her chest and held on to
him like he was about to be swept up by a current.
I wasn't surprised by her reaction. Every time I
entered the same room as her, she'd tense up. Her
bug eyes would expand like she feared for her life.

Because I didn't want to leave any child out, I
suggested an alternative. "If everyone can't go, can
we at least have popcorn and watch a movie?"

Clara sighed in frustration. She knew what her
sister was up to just as well as I did. "Popcorn and
a movie is good. I'll start popping."

I held out my hand to stop her. "I got it." She did
so much already that I wanted her to sit back and
chill like she was doing.

Not only was the kitchen right behind the wall
of the dining room, but I hadn't made it out of
the room good before Aunt Nora started with the
hate. "You all reckon this is safe? Her being here
and all, and around your boys?" Her thunderous,
raspy voice could fill an entire stadium without a
microphone.

"Eva is a good kid who's gone through a lot,"
Uncle Bobby responded. A little frustration laced
his tone as it did every time someone started in on
me.

Aunt Nora just had to dig her long, curled, bur-
gundy-painted claws in further. "Is it contagious?"

"Is what contagious?" Uncle Bobby asked.

"You know, whatever's wrong with her." Aunt Nora had no shame in her line of questioning, nor did she care if I heard.

It was an honor to hear Uncle Bobby come to my defense. "You sound ignorant, Nora. You know you can leave at any time if it bothers you this much."

I ran to the dining room when I heard the table rattle. Nora had jumped up, offended. Her cigarette bounced around between her lips as she muttered, "Don't call me when that crazy rubs off on you and your chirren." She made a beeline to the door with her oxygen tank in tow, running over a couple of feet along the way.

Soon after, the others started packing up and leaving. I hated that I was treated that way, but I was used to it. Still, I wondered why they came around if they were so bothered by me.

Uncle Bobby shook his head. He and Clara knew I wouldn't do anything to harm anyone physically. If they trusted me around their 11-year-old twins, why couldn't everyone else give me a fair chance? I wondered if they'd be better off without me. I was sick of being judged and tired of my aunt and uncle being harassed because of me. How many battles would they have to fight only to learn they'd never win the war?

My mission was to prove wrong those who questioned my sanity. They would see that I was a regular person. Sad, but regular.

First, I did what my mother always encouraged. I sought the Kingdom of God. After a long, deep prayer, she'd often splash oil around. Being that Clara was a pescatarian, she had plenty of it handy. I grabbed some from the kitchen and rushed back to my room before she noticed.

I knelt beside my bed, rested my knees on top of a plush pillow, and squeezed my hands together. For some reason, I was afraid that if I broke my prayer stance before I said, "Amen," my words would fall back down to earth. My request had to be heard.

"Dear Lord. Please fix me. If you can't fix me, then please fix those who look at me weirdly instead of as the beautiful girl you created me to be. Amen." I unfolded my hands and saw stars when I opened my eyes. But then I remembered something important. I returned to my praying position. "Lord, I miss my mother and brother so much. If it's not too much trouble, can you please tell them hello for me? Thank you. Amen." My heart ached not having them around, especially Michael. I wasn't as sad when he was here.

Feeling good about what I had accomplished, I splashed some oil around the room for finality. For days, my room reeked. And for days, I waited. Nothing changed. Despair still surrounded me, and spectators' eyes still judged. Then I remembered how skilled my mother was when praying,

and if it didn't work for her, it wouldn't work for a
novice like myself.

On to plan B. I decided to take matters into
my own hands. Uncle Bobby and Clara were kind
to me, and I wanted to be equally kind to them.
I wanted to be that girl they never had due to
complications Clara experienced after giving birth
to the twins. I figured I could just double up on my
meds to make it work faster. I started taking two
pills every day instead of just the one prescribed.
Although things changed, it wasn't the change I
had hoped for. My appetite decreased while the
amount of sleep I got increased. And instead of
racing the twins downstairs to the breakfast table
each morning, I lagged, if I came out of my room
at all. The desire to live faded, and what people
thought of me was no longer any of my concern.

The pills weren't working. After doing a little
research to find out why my meds weren't making
me happy, or at minimum, less sad, I learned
suicidal thoughts were a side effect of certain an-
tidepressants. What kind of sense did that make?

I felt as if I had entered a lonely place. It must
have been the same place my mother entered when
she lost her kids. I didn't just feel like I wanted to
die. I had a plan. A combination of Uncle Bobby's
blood pressure meds mixed with whatever Clara
took and something over the counter would do
the trick. It would be painless. I would drift off

to a permanent sleep and not feel the emptiness anymore. Plus, I'd be reunited with my mother and brother, where I belonged.

The thought of what my death would do to the people who had taken me in made me sick to my stomach. I knew the pain of losing a loved one to suicide, and I didn't want to hurt anyone else like that, but what choice did I have? Uncle Bobby and Clara deserved better, and I was too ashamed to ask for help. I was better off gone.

Unlike my mother, I didn't leave a note. Notes made things worse.

My suicide attempt failed.

Clara came into my room and found me with a faint pulse. She called the ambulance and remained by my side while I was in the hospital.

"The Lord just placed it on my heart to check on you before I called it a night," Clara said right before I was transferred from the bed to a wheelchair. Her words were soothing through her always-soft-spoken voice. I knew she cared for me, and I knew it hurt her to find me unresponsive. "We are going to get through this." She gently rubbed my back as I was wheeled away to the psychiatric part of the hospital.

My stomach burned from being pumped. That alone should've been a surefire deterrent to suicide. Admittedly, it wasn't. Even with the outpatient follow-up care that the hospital had arranged for me, I still wasn't happy. The new medicine didn't work either. Every time I alerted the clinic staff, they'd say, "Give it time."

I gave it time.

And more time.

Years later, I still struggled to be right. I had accepted defeat and gave up trying to convince everyone, including myself, that it was "just depression" and that I would somehow grow out of it. Disorders of the mind weren't accepted or understood and never would be.

I'd let Uncle Bobby and Clara down so many times that I was surprised they hung in there with me. I just knew that when my eighteenth birthday came around, they'd have my bags packed and waiting at the door. Only, they didn't. Then I became convinced it would happen on my twenty-first birthday.

"Happy birthday!" the four of them screamed when I finally emerged from my room for dinner after sleeping all day.

I broke down in tears. "Thank you," I said, relieved. I had been anticipating which park benches I'd sleep on and what shelters would take in a person like me. If all else failed, I'd purposely go crazy. At least at the psych ward, I'd have a bed and food.

Clara hadn't changed a bit. She was right there to console me. "Oh, dear. It's your birthday. You can't cry on your day."

"Tears of joy," I said. There was joy in knowing that I'd still have a roof over my head.

Uncle Bobby pushed a small, neatly wrapped box in my direction. I'd never seen him smile so hard, but he exposed his new set of dentures. "Go on, open it," he encouraged me.

My heart pounded, and my hands shook, thinking the contents inside would be an eviction letter. I nervously held it until my uncle instructed me to open it again. They'd always celebrated my birthday and gotten me something, but this time seemed different. They'd never been this excited. The twins even jumped up and down. Was everyone ready for me to leave?

"Hurry up!" one of the twins shouted.

A Toyota key stared back at me when I flipped the top open. I gasped, thinking I understood, but I was not quite sure I understood. Was the car my new home? "What?" I shook my head, confused.

"Surprise!" everyone shouted in unison.

"A car? You guys got me a car?"

Clara folded her hands under her chin and beamed.

"But . . ." I covered my mouth and gurgled the rest of my words. "I don't go anywhere."

"We are hoping that will change," Uncle Bobby said.

Clara's long, bone-straight black hair swayed with her nod. "We think you need to get out, smell the air, make some friends, and live. There is so much more to life than being cooped up in a tiny room all day, looking at the same four walls. You've done that long enough."

Maybe there was more to life for them. They were regular and could function. I was not.

I was surprised to hear Clara say that anyway. She and Uncle Bobby made a lot of decisions to ensure I stayed away from harmful people. Isolation became my comfort zone. Because of my issues, Uncle Bobby and Clara felt homeschooling was the better option for me, so I never made friends, and even before my life changed, Michael was my only friend. The back porch was the closest place I went for fresh air. And if I left the neighborhood, it was always with my family. I was comfortable being inside. I felt safe. I felt unjudged.

"I don't know what to say." I wept into the collar of my pajama shirt.

"Wanna take it for a spin?" Uncle Bobby asked.

"Let me change real quick." I dashed upstairs, took the quickest shower, sprayed an abundance of peach body mist on, and even combed my hair for the first time in weeks. I had to look right for my first time driving my own car.

About thirty minutes later, Uncle Bobby hopped in the passenger seat while Clara and the twins piled in the back.

I drove us to get ice cream, and after I whipped the car into the driveway, lightly bumping a shrub in the process, I ran to my room and dove into my bed, kicking my legs like I was treading water. If my mother hadn't taught me to drive or taken me to get my license before she died, that car would have been a waste. I smiled harder, reminiscing over the many times my brother snuck and let me drive our mother's car even before she did. I sighed at the thought of missing them.

"Congratulations!" interrupted my celebration.

I froze for a second. I didn't recognize that voice, and who would be in my room at this time of night? I shook away that thought after I looked around and didn't see anyone. All the excitement had me tripping, but then it happened again.

"Congratulations! Happy."

I jumped from the bed and tiptoed to my door. 'Twins?" I whispered through the crack out into the hallway.

"No," the unidentifiable voice answered, sounding like it was at a distance.

My eyes widened. "Who's in here?" I asked as I clicked on the light and ran to turn on my desk lamp.

The voice giggled. *"A friend."*

I bolted into the hall and stayed there for hours. Whatever I did, I knew I couldn't tell Uncle Bobby and Clara. My car would surely be my home. Once

I calmed down, I eased back into my abode to grab a pillow and blanket. Even though I had shifted to the couch, I still felt a need to watch my back. Eventually, I drifted off to sleep, only to be awakened by another faint whisper.

"Eva."

I jumped up, swinging, and caught Uncle Bobby in the arm.

"Whoa! Whoa!" he shouted, trying to hold my arms.

When I realized it was him, I fell back onto the sofa, panting and sweating.

"Bad dream?" he asked, breathing hard himself.

I nodded. "I'm so sorry. I would never—"

He held his hands up to silence me. "I know you wouldn't do anything to hurt me." He hugged me tightly.

"So you're not kicking me out?" My lips were pressed into his armpit, so the question came out muffled.

Uncle Bobby looked hurt by what I asked. His head hung low and moved from side to side. "What? What would make you say that? No one is kicking you out. You can stay here as long as you want or need."

I hoped he meant that, because I never saw myself being on my own. Lord only knew what would happen to me after he and Clara transitioned. "Thank you, Uncle Bobby. You and Clara have been so good to me, and I know I'm not the easiest person to deal with."

Uncle Bobby laughed. "Nonsense. Continue to work hard to stay healthy, and things will turn around. Speaking of which, the pharmacy called the landline. They finally got everything worked out with the insurance. Your refills are ready."

Then it hit me. Because of a mix-up between the pharmacy and insurance company, I hadn't had my medicine in a few days. That explained the voice.

"Why don't you drive that new car of yours to the pharmacy and pick it up?"

If my eyes weren't attached, they would have popped out of the sockets and rolled around the floor. "By myself?"

"Why not? What's the point of having a car if you can't just go?"

"Oh, my God, Uncle Bobby. Thank you so much." I almost cut off the poor man's circulation with how hard I squeezed his neck. I had a license, but I had never driven anywhere alone, always supervised. I was scared but more excited than anything. They really did trust me and love me.

"Be careful. Signal, and double-check your blind spot," Uncle Bobby reminded me.

"I will," I yelled. I was almost to my room before he got it out. Funny how the excitement made me forget all about the monster that had whispered to me the night before.

Entry 6

Dear Diary:

"Eva Moss?" I was greeted from behind.

I knew who it was before I turned around. His voice was still recognizable. When I turned around, he stepped back and took in every essence of my being. My five-foot-seven-inch, size-six frame hadn't changed much since we last saw each other. There was a little weight gain because of the anti-depressant, but it was nothing to frown upon. By the way he looked at me, I could tell that he still hadn't lost his lust for me after so many years.

For the first time, I felt something too. It was an immediate attraction, but not because of his good looks. What attracted me to him was the way he made me feel inside. "Myles," I finally uttered. I was surprised by his attire. No animals. No flames. Nothing immature with what he wore. He looked fancy in the gray Italian-cut suit, blue dress shirt, and matching tie. His cologne swiveled around my nose even at a distance.

"How have you been?" he asked and tried to lean in for a hug, but I took a step back.

It took me a minute to answer. A burning sensation lurked inside of me. It felt like Freddy Krueger himself scratched to be freed. It hurt and felt good at the same time. The whispering monster was back. I tried my best to ignore it, but I didn't know how much longer I could hold on.

"You look amazing. I didn't think you could have grown to be prettier than you were in high school, but I have never been more wrong," Myles added when I didn't answer the initial question.

My heart felt as if it would burst through my chest. "Um . . . I . . . um . . ."

The intercom sounded. "Pickup for Moss."

Without a goodbye, I turned and rushed to the counter, hoping Myles would have disappeared, but when I finished my transaction, he was still there. I attempted to walk past him as if I didn't see him, but he stopped me.

"Hold on a second." When his fingers touched my forearm to slow me down, a surge went through me. I thought I was going to pass out.

"I'm sorry, Myles. I really have to go. It was good to see you, though."

Dismissing him didn't work. He wouldn't take no for an answer, just like before.

"I thought I'd never see you again." Myles took a step back. "You are even more beautiful now than you were back then," he told me again.

Although my face wore a frown, my heart smiled. No one from the opposite sex had ever complimented me like this before.

"You know I've had a crush on you since school," Myles added. "And seeing you today, it hasn't changed." Myles smiled, and when I didn't say anything, he continued talking. "I've tried looking you up on social media, but I couldn't find you. You were private back then, so I figured it was the same now."

I awkwardly rocked from side to side. "Yeah, I'm still pretty private."

"You still live in this area?"

I stole a glance, nodded, and then returned my attention to the triangle-shaped floor tiles. This man sent electric shocks through my body, and if I didn't get away from him, he would be picking me up off these triangles.

"That's cool. I'm visiting my parents and stopped in to grab their medicine. I figured you would have moved away too with all that happened." Myles realized his slip. He bit his lip and tightly closed his eyes. "I'm sorry," he apologized, shaking his head.

All that happened. He meant because he killed my brother. Everything around me seemed to stand still. My eyes strayed back to the floor and traced over the shape of the triangles once more. *Or does he know I am crazy?*

"I'm sorry about your mom, by the way. She was the best."

If he knew about my mom, then he knew about me.

"I'm sorry if this is too forward, but can I call you?" he asked. "Maybe we can catch up."

"I don't have a phone," I lied.

Myles nodded and pointed. "Well, what is that in your hand?"

Dang.

"Look, Myles, I appreciate the interest—"

"Uh-oh." He took a step back. "Let me down easy."

"I don't think it would be a wise thing to do, that's all."

"I understand. But still, take my number in case you want to catch up."

I sighed out, "Okay."

"Can I program it in that phone that's not yours?" he laughed, and so did someone else.

I spun around and kept spinning, trying to see who was listening. It was just Myles and I from what I could see. "Did you hear that?" I asked.

"What? The sound of rejection?"

I ignored him and peeked down the aisle to the left and right of us.

"Is everything okay?" Myles asked.

"Say yes," someone instructed me.

I gasped and jumped back, knocking over the endcap bookcase. I didn't bother to clean it up. I had to get home.

When I rushed off, the pharmacy aisles became a maze. I was a mouse trying to find my way out. HAND AND BODY LOTION. SKIN CARE. ACNE. The large white lettering that sat atop a gray background, accented with red numbers, that hung from the ceiling only confused me more. This CVS was practically my hangout spot, yet I couldn't navigate my way out.

"Where's the exit?" Sweat snuck from underneath my bra. The ten rolls of deodorant under each arm were no match for the perspiration that immediately had me smelling like mildew.

I turned down another aisle. "Allergy. Children's health. Cold remedies." Everything was hazy. I kept going. "Deodorant. Bath care. Sanitary." There was the pharmacy again. I reversed my feet and backed into Myles.

My hands fumbled the white paper bag, and my heartbeat amplified. "Jesus, Myles, you scared me."

"I'm sorry." He bent down and picked up my two medicine bags, which were stapled together. "What are you looking for? I can help."

One of the bags ripped when I snatched it from Myles's hand. "I got it. I don't need anything from you." I didn't mean to snap, but those bags held sensitive information and were none of his business.

A worried expression spread across his face. "Are you okay, Eva?"

What was I supposed to say? "I think I hear voices, and I'm lost in a square space that has one way in and one way out"? A blind person could have made it to the exit before me. All I had to do was face the opposite direction of the pharmacy and walk outside as I had done many times before. For some reason, my brain and body wouldn't coordinate.

"Well, can I at least walk you to your car?"

My tongue touched the roof of my mouth, preparing to tell Myles no, but the muffled whispers stopped me.

"Say yes."

"What? Absolutely not," I countered. I thought I heard that right. I thought the whisper instructed me to allow Myles to walk me.

"I'm sorry. I didn't mean to offend you," he apologized, which was all he'd done since he spotted me, it seemed.

"I wasn't talking to you, Myles." That slipped out.

Myles took in the scenery around us, almost completing a full circle. He turned back to me and said, "Unless you see dead people, we are the only two standing here."

It wasn't that I could see them. I *thought* I could hear them.

Myles tapped my shoulder, interrupting my focus on the now-multiple inaudible whispers that wouldn't stop. Occasionally, one would come in clearly. *"Give me lipstick,"* I thought I heard.

I snapped over the random statement. "That makes no sense."

"I'm sorry. I wasn't trying to be insensitive. It was intended to be a joke," Myles said.

"What?" I snapped again.

"Is that 'what' for me this time?" he cautiously asked.

My hair was soggy. That was how badly I had started sweating. "I'm not feeling well, so I'm going to go. Good seeing you." I waved and was supposed to walk off, but the instructions from one of the whispering voices was unmistakable.

"Let him walk you." This time the voice was familiar.

"Michael?" I asked aloud.

Myles blinked back tears. "I'm . . . I'm sorry."

"I'm sorry too," I said and power walked toward the exit by myself.

Entry 7

Dear Diary:

Luckily, it was only a three-minute drive home. I raised the stereo's volume as loud as it would go to drown out the whispers. The louder the radio went, the louder Michael's voice became. I sped, swerving in and out of traffic, trying to cut three minutes down to sixty seconds.

I whipped my car into the driveway, this time running into the bushes and knocking off the side mirror of my car. I rushed into the house, heading to my room to hopefully hide from what was happening, but I was stopped by Uncle Bobby.

"How was your drive?" he asked.

"Fine," I lied and tried to speed past him.

"Hold on there." Uncle Bobby looked me up and down as if he sensed something was off. "You need me to help carry some bags?"

"I only went to the pharmacy. There are no bags."

"Every woman I know goes to the store for one thing and comes out with bags full of stuff," he said through giggles. "Unless you're hiding them in your trunk." He tossed another questioning glare my way.

"Not this woman. May I be excused?"

He peered over his reading glasses. "You sure you're okay?"

I nodded.

When I made it to my room, I locked the door behind me. "What in the hell is going on?" I paced and convinced myself the voices had started because of the missed doses. At that moment, I thought about swallowing two to make up for it, but I refused to have my stomach pumped again.

I settled my nerves but got riled up again while heading to survey the damage to my car. What were Uncle Bobby and Clara going to say? I was worried they'd take my car, and if they did, I was sure I deserved it. They had been too good to me to deceive them, but I couldn't tell them why I hit the bushes. My hospital admissions had diminished, and with them getting me a car, that meant I was on the right track to independence. Approaching them with, "Hey, guys, I am starting to hear voices," would not help them continue to trust that I was capable of roaming freely without them worrying about my well-being.

The mirror dangled, and a few scratches surrounded the speck of missing paint. Nothing a little Gorilla Glue couldn't fix.

"Eva."

Oh, hell no! Not again. I knew that voice, and
it happened to be living. I threw both hands on
my hips and stiffly turned around. "What are you
doing here, Myles?" I imagined my face was as red
as my car.

He held his hands out like he didn't want the
problems my body language expressed. "I'm sorry
to pop up like this, but I was worried about you."

"How did you know I'd be here, Myles?"

"I didn't," he eased out. "I didn't know if your
uncle still lived here, but I took a chance. I don't
mean any harm. I was at my parents' and couldn't
stop thinking about what happened at the pharmacy. I just wanted to make sure you were okay."

Sweet gesture. Still, Myles shouldn't have un-
expectedly popped up. Instead of wasting time
explaining that to him, I pivoted to head inside.
Once he saw my back, he would understand.

He landed on the porch the same time I did.

"What are you doing? Your car is that way." I
pointed.

"I just . . . I want . . ." He closed his eyes and
sharply inhaled. "Michael."

I heaved a breath hearing him say my brother's
name.

"I never got the chance to apologize. I know
that won't change what happened, but . . ." Myles
buckled over and bawled. I watched as his hands
trembled against his knees.

Maybe I could've been a little sympathetic, possibly even consoled him. Myles was too much of a negative reminder. It hurt looking at him. I stuck two fingers under his chin to lift his face so he could look me in the eyes when I told him, "Don't ever come back here."

His confused eyes were red. I imagined them to be the same shade of red that poured out of my brother when he flew through the windshield of Myles's car. As much as I wanted to shield myself from the details, one bored day, I became bold enough to look online. There were pictures of the mangled, overturned Jeep. The airbags had deployed, and the windows were shattered. Obviously, the maple tree won. I squinted, trying to see if I could see Michael's lifeless body anywhere in the pictures.

"I understand," Myles finally responded. He reached for the handle of the screen door, but I swatted his hand away.

"Go!" I demanded.

"I wouldn't do that if I were you."

I covered my ears like that action would silence Michael's voice in my head. I had to send Myles away for multiple reasons. Pain, mainly. But also because I wasn't sure how my family would receive him after killing my brother.

"Stop him."

"No!" I yelled.

Of course, Myles thought I was talking to him and slowed his pace.

I shooed him. "Bye." I knew the poor fella was confused, but so was I.

Uncle Bobby's gruff voice penetrated the atmosphere. "Well, look what the wind blew in," he said, stepping onto the porch.

Myles's eyes lit up. "How you doing, Mr. Bobby?" Although his tone was somber, he seemed genuinely excited that he had a chance to see Uncle Bobby after all these years.

Uncle Bobby dropped down in his rocking chair. "Getting old but can't complain." He patted his knee. "This old thing here tends to give me trouble now and again. A little gout. Nothing I can't handle."

Myles trudged up the stairs as if he were invited and shook Uncle Bobby's hand. My uncle held on to Myles, and I was terrified at what would happen next.

"Can I get you a cold beer, young man?" he gently offered.

"Uncle Bobby," I called and growled at the same time. Why bring up alcohol when that was why Michael died in the first place? Myles was required to maintain his sobriety. I learned that online, too.

Myles lowered his eyes for obvious reasons. "No, sir. I don't drink."

Uncle Bobby let out a grunt and continued making small talk that made me extra uncomfortable. "I haven't seen you since before"—he paused for a second— "since before Michael passed. How have you been doing with that?" He rocked back and forth in the rickety rocking chair and studied Myles.

I cringed, nervous and embarrassed for my brother's former partner in crime. I plopped down on the wooden porch bench and buried my face within my hands. This wasn't going to end well. Myles should have left me alone like I warned him.

Myles's normal bronze skin tone lightened two shades. "I'm doing, Mr. Bobby."

"Just doing? What does that mean?"

Myles cleared his throat, wiped his forehead, and then stuffed his hands in his slacks. He slid one foot back on a step like he was about to descend abruptly. "I am sorry for everything, sir. I want to speak with you man-to-man and do whatever I can to earn your forgiveness if you allow me the opportunity." Myles turned to me and added, "And, Eva, I'd like the same opportunity with you, if that's okay?"

I stared at Uncle Bobby. I didn't know what to say. Was it okay?

"I swear, I never meant for that to happen to Michael. I—"

Uncle Bobby silenced him. "I know that, son. I've been in your shoes before. I used to think I was invincible when I was your age. In fact, there was this hole-in-the-wall bar on Fifteenth Street. I shut it down every night," he laughed, reminiscing about his partying days. "Every night, me and the guys would run up a tab, shoot pool, and play darts. I'd stagger out of the bar and swerve the whole way home. I got two DUIs. It was Clara who tamed me. But I could have very well taken a life, if not my own."

The size of my eyes drastically grew. I never knew that about my uncle. To me, he was practically a saint.

"I appreciate you sharing that with me, Mr. Bobby. You were lucky. My actions did take a life, and it's tough. An everyday struggle. I'd still like to own up to my responsibility, however. Whatever you all need, if you will allow it."

My uncle slowed his rocking. "I appreciate you stepping up like this. It's admirable. It's okay with me as long as it's okay with Eva."

Both men looked at me, awaiting a response, awaiting easy forgiveness like my uncle gave. I wasn't quite there yet and wasn't sure if I'd ever be.

"It's okay," Michael whispered.

I shook my head at my brother's request. "Not now. Please leave me alone."

"I'm sorry," Myles apologized for the hundredth time.

Uncle Bobby looked at me like he may have been a bit disappointed in the way I responded. "True healing begins where forgiveness starts. Give the young man a chance, and stop being so harsh," he said.

Myles still didn't give up. At least not with Uncle Bobby. "Maybe we can cast our lines, sir?"

Uncle Bobby got excited. "Shoot, boy, you ain't saying nothing. We can go now."

Myles laughed. "I was hoping I could take Eva out this evening, but I understand if she needs more time." After a lingering silence, he added, "I'm willing to wait as long as I need to."

Uncle Bobby watched a car pass before asking, "Out where?"

"Nothing fancy," Myles replied. "Maybe dinner and a movie. Or whatever she wants."

"Sit awhile." Uncle Bobby motioned to the rocking chair beside him.

I thought I swallowed all my teeth. Why wouldn't Myles just go? I'd warned him more than one time.

"Let him stay." Michael's voice boomed through my ears as if he were scolding me for not listening to him.

I jumped at how loud and clear he'd come through. Both Myles and my uncle frowned as they looked at me.

"Something bit me," I lied, leaning over and scratching my ankle.

"Stay. Stay. Stay," Michael chanted even louder.

I covered my ears. "Why are you so loud?"

Again, both men looked at me like I was crazy. They would have been right.

Once again, Myles apologized. "I'm sorry, Eva. I wasn't trying to disturb you."

The way Uncle Bobby looked at me, I knew he wasn't pleased with my rudeness. "I just have a slight headache," I lied.

"I can run to the store and get something for you to take if you want," Myles offered.

Before I could answer, Uncle Bobby chimed in, "Eva, run upstairs and grab my cigar box, please. And some waters."

That was Uncle Bobby's way of getting rid of me. He pretended to be pleasant but was going to say something mean to Myles and didn't want me to hear. Typical Uncle Bobby. Mr. Nice Guy image around us, but there was another side to him. A rough version that didn't come out unless he was playing protector. Anytime he needed to say something that would tarnish the way we looked at him, he'd send us on an errand. I caught him once. Stopped shy of entering a room where he dog walked one of his so-called friends for making advances at Clara. I never saw the man again after that. Still, Uncle Bobby was a saint to me. What concerned me was if he'd noticed I was in the middle of a breakdown and wanted to send me off before I acted any crazier, or if he planned to tell Myles my secret.

Both of them were quiet when I came back. The bottle of water rattled in Myles's hand every time he picked it up to take a sip, so whatever Uncle Bobby said terrified him.

"What went on while I was gone?"

"Man talk, between us men." Uncle Bobby left it at that, and so did I. He lit his cigar and took a drag.

Myles and Uncle Bobby puffed and talked sports. I didn't know anything about either of the things they had going on. I listened to them and Michael. Yesterday, his voice scared me. Although it was weird, I had started to grow giddy hearing from him.

"Eva, listen," Michael whispered. *"If this is going to work, you have to keep me a secret. They won't understand."*

"How?" I blurted out, already failing the mission.

Uncle Bobby and Myles looked at me again. Confusion seemed to double on their faces.

I tried cleaning it up. "How do y'all know so much about sports? I find it uninteresting."

"Hard to explain," Uncle Bobby said, along with a few other things that were overshadowed by Michael's whispers.

"Only nod or think when in company. I'll under-stand."

"Well, I am going to get going," Myles announced. He put out his cigar and left the cap in the ashtray. "Thank you so much for this, Mr. Bobby."

"Anytime, son."

"Eva, I hope to see you soon. Is it okay for me to call you tomorrow?"

"Yes," Michael answered on my behalf. Good thing I was the only one who could hear him.

"Maybe we can grab lunch," Myles added over my silence and Michael's repeated push.

"Yes," my brother said again.

Myles and I exchanged numbers, and Michael was pleased.

Before Myles reached his car, he turned and said, "Oh, and, Eva, happy belated birthday."

He remembered?

Uncle Bobby and I watched as he climbed into his Hummer and slowly drove away.

I exhaled. "That was awkward."

"You think so?"

"Definitely."

"Probably more awkward for him," Uncle Bobby said.

"Why is that? Did you tell him I was crazy?"

"Not my story to tell, and stop using that word for yourself or you will become that." Uncle Bobby shrugged and offered me a cigar, knowing I didn't smoke. "Myles has always been a good kid. I heard you out here sassing him, so I intervened."

"I was not doing anything to that man," I protested. "He had no business coming over here without permission."

"The boy's eyes are sad. He's been wearing this weight on him for all these years. He needed this moment to get it out."

"What about me and how I feel? I associate him with loss. It's hard enough already."

Uncle Bobby nodded his understanding. "He's paid his debt to society."

"But he hasn't paid his debt to me," I countered.

"Avenge me."

When Michael whispered that, his sudden presence made sense. Everyone tried endlessly to convince me that my brother was gone for good, but I knew he wouldn't leave me. If revenge was what he wanted, then revenge was what he would get.

Entry 8

Dear Diary:

It was weird for my phone to ring, let alone at night. Other than the scammers calling to remind me that my car warranty had expired, Uncle Bobby, Clara, and the twins were the only people who had my number, and there was rarely a need to call because I was always home.

It was late when Myles's name flashed across my screen. Well, late for me. I was usually in bed no later than nine. It was after ten when I felt the vibration against my mattress.

"Yes?" I groggily answered.

"Did I wake you?" Myles asked.

Instead of answering with the obvious, I asked, "What's up? Is something wrong?"

He stuttered a bit before responding, "There is something I need to say to you."

I groaned. I knew I should've ignored his call, but that wasn't what Michael wanted. "Okay. I'm listening."

"It's about Michael."

I sat up. It felt like my large intestines and small intestines switched places. Did he know? "Go on," I eagerly encouraged him.

"I want to make sure you hear me and understand how sorry I am."

I had a little more energy in my voice when I said, "I'm listening."

Myles inhaled and gave his speech. "Not making excuses or anything, but I was young, and we were just trying to have some fun before we left for college. There's not a day that goes by that I don't think about him or the hurt I caused. I miss Michael. I often wonder what NFL team he would have played for. Would it have been the Falcons? I wonder if he would have actually found a girl to settle down with or if he would have been a polygamist like he used to say."

I laughed, remembering my brother and his foolish girl talk. Football talk, too.

Myles sniffed and sucked in some air. "I never thought I would cause the death of my best friend. I never thought I'd crash my car. Life wasn't supposed to be like this. I swear on everything I love, I never meant for that to happen, and I'm sorry. I wish I could trade places with Michael."

You will, I thought but then scolded myself. "Avenge" could mean so many things, not necessarily death. Besides, I was no killer, and I knew Michael wouldn't expect me to do anything like that.

"Michael was my brother too," Myles continued. "Not by blood, but he was my brother. I'm sorry."

How many times was this man going to apologize? "It's fine, Myles." It was fine because Michael said it was.

"I should have made a better effort to find you and make amends a long time ago. I could have stopped by Mr. Bobby's long before now. But when I saw you at the pharmacy, I took it as an answered prayer."

I was speechless.

"I'm sorry for waking you and sorry if I upset you with what I said."

Still, not a word from me.

"I'll give you some space, but if you ever want to talk or feel up to going out, please call me."

When we hung up, I stared at the brightness of my phone until it automatically locked. Then I stared at the black screen, replaying Myles's words. The inaudible whispers started, but they didn't scare me this time. I had confirmation that Michael was mixed within the whispers because they put me right to sleep like a lullaby. Like Bedtime Stories by Michael used to do.

It must've been destiny, because Clara brought Myles up the next morning at breakfast. "Bobby told me you've reconnected with Myles."

My head slowly rolled in Uncle Bobby's direction. "Clara, how does it feel to be married to a snitch?" I jokingly asked.

We had cried enough together. It felt good to laugh as a family.

My laughter subsided when Clara suggested, "You should invite him over for dinner."

"That won't be necessary," I responded.

"Do you like him?" Clara pried. She poured herself some of that fancy tea she drank and plopped beside me with more questions. "Has he asked you out on a date yet?" Her face lit up like a proud mom of a daughter who potentially had her first boyfriend.

I shrugged. Had they forgotten about who Myles was? What about the damage he had caused? Why were they so eager for us to connect?

Clara pried more. "What's holding you back? If you like him, give him a chance. I remember he was always so sweet on you."

I had started to become overwhelmed by her questions. I fidgeted every time she asked one.

Uncle Bobby peered over his glasses. "Leave the girl alone. You see she doesn't want to talk about it."

Although I wanted the conversation to end, Clara was happy to have boy talk with me, and for everything she had done for me, maybe this would be a way to repay her. "It's okay, Uncle Bobby. I don't like Myles, Clara. You know, because of . . ." The light, uncomfortable smile substituted for the obvious.

Clara reached over and rubbed my shoulder. "Oh, sweetheart. I'm sorry. I understand. I was only asking because your mom used to tell me you and Myles would end up married."

My eyes crossed. "What?"

Clara nodded, looking off into space. My mother and Clara were sisters through marriage, but everyone thought they were biologically related as close as they were. Michael's death hurt her, but my mother's death changed her. She was still a sweet lady but different. She zoned out a lot, and I started to wonder if my mother talked to her like Michael spoke to me.

"I'm sure if I ever tried to marry anybody, Uncle Bobby would run them off."

My uncle's eyes widened. "Who's the snitch now?"

Clara scowled at Uncle Bobby. "What did you do, Bobby?"

"Not a thing," he said as a smirk reconstructed his lips.

"Bobby," Clara growled louder than a hungry lion.

"I just told the boy if he wanted to date my niece, he'd better have his stuff together."

"Just like that? In that tone? With that exact language?" Clara asked.

When Uncle Bobby cleared his throat, we all knew the answers to those questions.

"Bobby!" Clara shouted his name.

"Okay," he said. "I may not have said 'stuff.' There may have been a few threats." He gave a half shrug.

"And?" Clara asked, seemingly not convinced he had given the whole truth.

"And nothing. I've always liked the boy. I don't like what he did, but it was an accident. Us being mad at him forever won't bring Michael back. You can look at the boy and tell he's still reeling with guilt. He even said so himself. I believe him. His coming around is fine with me. Now, may I get back to my breakfast?"

Clara looked at me and said, "Invite him over for dinner Sunday."

"Invite him," Michael agreed.

With that assurance, I did.

Entry 9

Dear Diary:

After Myles ate dinner with my family and me, Michael provided clear instructions. *"Get close to him."*

I nodded as he had suggested when people were around.

"I have the blueprint for Myles's fate, Eva. Listen to me."

I nodded again, desperately wanting to know what he meant since I couldn't ask. Eyes squinted and eyebrows furrowed at my movements, but I did as my brother said. I thought it like he had also advised, but he gave no answers.

"I will instruct your moves for Myles. Listen to me, Eva. Avenge me."

I knew with the way I kept nodding that someone was bound to inquire, and I was right. "Eva, are you okay, dear?" Clara asked. She always paid close attention to my mood and body language. I think she thought she could catch the breakdown and stop it. I was sure she didn't want it to happen in front of Myles. Neither did I.

Things ended up moving rapidly for Myles and me. Within weeks, he had taken me to the movies and the beach. In all my life, I had never been to the beach. The only bodies of water I had been privileged to swim in were lakes with no sand and community pools.

"Myles Sanders, this . . ." I said as soon as my toes sank into the beach sand. I stood in awe, holding my hands out to my sides like I was a soaring bird. "This wind feels amazing. And this water"—I closed my eyes and inhaled—"it smells right."

Myles laughed. "How does water smell right?"

I shook my head at a loss for an intelligent explanation. "It just smells right. It doesn't smell like chlorine or pollution. It smells natural."

I wasn't the only one Myles thought about when it came to us spending time together. He'd even invited Uncle Bobby, Clara, and the twins out for a night of bowling. I'd never had so much fun in my life. Nor had I seen Uncle Bobby cut loose like he did. He danced to the bowling alley music, drank an entire pitcher of beer by himself, and beat all of us.

And Clara. The relieved expression on her face made my life. She had finally gotten a chance to sit back and enjoy herself. She didn't have to cater to anyone.

Myles's romantic gesture didn't stop with beach dates. One night, he surprised me by whisking me away on a helicopter ride, where we landed on the rooftop of a restaurant and dined on lobster and the most expensive fruit-infused water. Myles didn't drink because of his past troubles, and I didn't drink because I was told it would intensify the effects of my medication. Still, our water came in wineglasses, and we pretended.

"To us," Myles said and held his glass in the center of the table.

"To us." I smiled and followed suit. It was my first official toast.

"I have something I want to talk to you about," Myles said to me just before our lobsters arrived.

I held my breath, thinking he had figured out my secret. But how? I'd been cool. He couldn't have known. I eyed the bouquet of roses he'd given me when he picked me up for our date. Other than Myles dropping single roses on me in high school, no man had ever given me flowers before, and while I didn't know much about dating and relationships, I didn't see any man giving a woman flowers if that woman was hiding something from him. I couldn't tell him there was more to me than he knew. My skeletons were too intense to share in-depth with anyone who didn't have MD behind their name. Even with credentials, it was still tough to share.

I shook my head, prepared to be called out. "Myles, I—"

"Please don't reject me before I get it out," he interrupted.

"Go on," I said, hesitantly giving Myles the floor. My temples throbbed as I waited to hear him call me crazy.

"I have enjoyed spending time with you, and I was wondering if you'd be willing to split your time between my house and your family's house."

I exhaled. He didn't know about me. I leaned back in my chair both relieved and stunned. "Wh . . . what?"

"I know it hasn't been long since we've reconnected, but technically, we've known each other all our lives, so it's not like we are strangers. You don't have to move in right away. Just stay over sometimes. Build up to a permanent transition." When I didn't respond right away, Myles added, "No pressure. I would like for us to be exclusive, though."

Technically, we were strangers. I had other people inside me he'd never met. In fact, I was just beginning to meet them. And if I hid something that serious from Myles, I wondered what he hid from me. Plus, as much time as we spent together, we'd never really had in-depth discussions about life, goals, and especially illnesses.

I replayed Michael's instructions but had questions of my own. I was convinced Myles was up to something. "We've only been dating for two months. You want me to move in or stay over for sex? You do know I'm a virgin, right?"

Myles lightly choked on his water. "Eva, no. I would never. You are my best friend's sister. I have respect for you and him. We don't even have to sleep in the same bed or room. I have a guest room. You can have your own. Having your presence nearby is what matters most."

I blushed a little but didn't allow his gentlemanly behavior to melt me. "That's a big step, Myles."

"I know it is. Just think about it."

"There's a lot associated with me that you won't be able to handle," I warned him.

He slid the glass pitcher of fruit water from the center of the table so that nothing interfered with him looking into my eyes. He leaned in and whispered, "You let me be the judge of what I can and can't handle."

I was impressed with him and his response. That was the case with almost everything Myles said to me. From the moment I laid eyes on him, my heart beat faster with every word he spoke.

"Come home with me," he added.

Something dawned on me. "Where exactly do you live?" I asked, which was something else we'd never discussed.

"The Cambridge Lofts on Lake Oconee."

I smacked the table, amazed. "Get the hell out of here. Remember we used to fawn over the houses at that lake growing up?"

Myles smiled. "Yep. I loved going to y'all's family reunions, riding those jet skis, dreaming of being in a position to make money to afford a home there."

"And now you have one," I said, beaming with pride.

Myles nodded. "Great location. In between. A little over an hour from work in Atlanta and my parents in Hephzibah."

I knew it seemed silly and immature, but I hoped certain topics never came up. Specifically careers. Mainly because I didn't have one. I could look at Myles and tell he had something going for himself. His appearance reeked of businessman, and the way he handled business between two cell phones amazed me. I assumed that because he wanted things to work between us, he allowed me to control the flow. With that, there was a lot of avoidance on my end. Most of the time we spent together consisted of laughing and discussing whatever activity we did or whatever movie we watched. Serious discussions were bound to happen. I just hoped that once he found out I had nothing to offer, he'd still look at me the same.

"Where exactly is work?" I finally asked.

"I'm a sports agent at Rowe Sports and Entertainment Management. Day in and day out, I negotiate deals for athletes. Keeps me busy, but I love it."

"Wow! You accomplished that, too?" I raved, remembering his and Michael's plans. Michael was going to be the football player, and Myles would be the agent who negotiated all the deals for him, including Wheaties. My brother didn't even like that cereal, but he was convinced they'd endorse him over his good looks alone, which would increase his number of ladies.

"What about you? What do you do for work?" Myles asked the dreaded question. "If memory serves me correctly, you wanted to be a writer, producer, and film director, right?"

I fanned away his inquiries. "Nothing much. A little work-from-home writing job. Nothing as exciting as you," I lied and shifted the focus back on him before he pried anymore. "I am so proud of you, Myles. You have done everything you planned." I was proud but also a little jealous. Furthering my education was something I always longed for. However, my mental health derailed my college dreams to study creative writing and film. I barely graduated as a homeschooled student, and I doubted I'd have the educational or social skills needed to thrive in a college setting or the film industry.

I didn't think men blushed, but Myles did. His cheeks lit up like a little girl had asked if she could practice putting makeup on his face. "Thank you. That means a lot coming from you."

I tried my best to keep the focus on him and his accomplishments. "I still cannot believe you have a home on our favorite lake."

"And you can too if you want." He eyed me and sipped his water as if that action would make me immediately agree to his request.

Honestly, it did, though. I gave a half shrug as I thought that this would be my only opportunity to experience being on the other side of that lake every day. I downplayed my excitement with a slight, unenthusiastic smile. "I guess I can try," I bashfully said.

After dinner, Myles took me on a tour of his condo. When I walked into the massive open-floor plan, the first thing I noticed was the framed certificate of completion for drug and alcohol treatment. Michael would be proud.

"What's this?" I asked, noticing another frame. It was a picture of Myles standing with a group of younger kids.

He smiled. "Those are the kids in my mentoring program."

"Mentoring program?"

"Yeah." His eyes became glossy. "One Saturday a month, using my own experience, I mentor teenage boys on the importance of not drinking and driving."

I stared at Myles. No words, just a smile. Michael would definitely be proud.

I got comfy on the leather theater-style sectional couch, feeling blissful. Who knew a routine trip to the pharmacy would change my life? I had made peace with living the rest of my days in a bedroom of Uncle Bobby and Clara's home, never being able to experience what it was like to have a place of my own, get married, or start a family. How could I say no to all that changing?

The first goal that Michael set for me had been accomplished. Myles and I were close, official, and practically living together.

Entry 10

Dear Diary:

I enjoyed spending time with Myles, but I missed my brother. Surprisingly, the unpleasant urges I had experienced during my reunion with Myles were gone, and so was Michael. Before he jetted off to an undisclosed location, he left me with more instructions. *"Take meds as prescribed. Be back soon."*

Myles was supposed to be sacrificial, but I began to feel something different toward him. Something beautiful. I only knew of such beauty from the love displayed between Uncle Bobby and Clara. There were many nights I had gone into the kitchen for water and stumbled upon them snuggled up on the couch watching a movie. Then there were times when I'd overhear Uncle Bobby singing old-school tunes to Clara while they danced in the middle of the den. I had started to visualize Myles and me doing that.

Michael never mentioned these types of feelings surfacing within his plan. I wondered what he would have thought if he knew what brewed within me. Could he sense the feelings like he could understand my thoughts? I couldn't stop them. Anytime Myles was around, I felt butterflies flutter graciously throughout my stomach. I knew I wasn't supposed to fall in love, but Myles was such a gentleman that it was hard not to. That never happened in school, so I was confused.

For once in my life, I felt like a human instead of a pill-popping psychopath. Soon, I was convinced that Myles was the medication I needed to remain healthy, and I stopped taking what I had been prescribed. My body didn't like that. It started to change. Sleep wasn't in my vocabulary. I stayed up for days at a time, binge-watching television and beginning arts-and-crafts projects that I never completed. My head constantly pounded like a nail being hit by a hammer. I tolerated it all because I refused to consume any more drugs.

There was some goodness in all the madness. Michael came back. When he did, life became a tug of war—Myles versus Michael—and unfortunately for me, I was the rope.

I committed to helping Michael, and I planned to follow through with it. I owed my brother for all the times he was there for me. Despite that loyalty, I wanted to love them both. Michael hated Myles, and I understood why. I just didn't feel the same. I hoped to gather enough courage to convince

Michael of how different Myles was. Maybe he'd change his mind and we could figure out a way to move forward or at least happily coexist.

I was too afraid to embrace what I felt for Myles out of fear of my brother's reaction. I struggled, trying to come up with a way to ask Michael to reconsider the plan. What would he think of me if he knew the reason why I wanted him to reconsider? He trusted me to do a job, and I couldn't let him down.

"Falling in love is not a part of the plan," I'd chant under my breath every time I started to feel those flutters in Myles's presence. Then I'd remind myself of how gorgeous butterflies were along with their transformation, just like Myles and me. We'd grown as individuals and were good together. We had become better versions of our younger selves, even me. Myles had that effect on me. He made me want more for myself. He made me want better. Michael would understand if I put it that way. I persuaded myself to tell him how I felt.

I didn't have to tell Michael anything. He knew. *"Getting close was not the plan,"* he repeatedly lashed out.

Between the stress of Michael scolding me, the fear of losing him, and the sudden interruption of my medication, my health continued to quickly decline. The sicker I became, the more talkative Michael was. He continuously and rapidly fired off demands.

"Get him," he laughed. It was an evil cackle that scared me.

"How, Michael?"

"Get him," he repeated and laughed again. *"Push him on the train tracks, set him on fire, put bleach in his drink. Get him. Get him. Get him. Do it."*

I grabbed a pencil and a notepad to write down the instructions. I barely made out what he said. His faint voice frustrated me. No matter how tight I gripped the pencil, I couldn't write one word. My hands trembled. Finally, the lead connected with the paper, allowing me to scribble illegible words.

"What's happening to me?" I yelled out. I flipped the pencil over and erased what I had written. Regardless of how fast and hard I tried, the words wouldn't disappear. My grip tightened on the pencil. I was determined to correct my mistakes, but the pencil snapped in two. That was all I needed to send me over the edge. I threw the pencil pieces across the room and paced, biting my nails and tasting blood in the process.

"Destroy him," Michael loudly demanded. I heard him clearly as his voice seemed to come through the television. *"Trick him. Destroy him."*

I became so enraged that I faced the TV and screamed, "Michael, please stop yelling at me."

"I'll leave," my brother threatened over my disobedience.

Of course, I didn't want that. I dropped to my knees and hugged the flat screen. "Please, don't leave. Please, I'll do whatever you want."

"What are you doing?" Myles asked from the doorway.

I forgot he was due back from a business trip. Our living arrangements worked perfectly. Myles was away for work a lot, making it easy to hide the real me. When he was here, most nights, we slept in different bedrooms. When we did share a bed, the most we ever did was cuddle and kiss.

"Lie," Michael whispered. His voice sounded as if he were far away instead of booming through the surround sound as before.

"I was praying," I lied.

Myles eased into the house, made his way to the remote, and lowered the volume. His eyes narrowed as he surveyed the mess I had made. "I could hear the TV from down the hall and you yelling over it."

Desperate to change the subject and feel the safety of being entangled in his arms, I jumped up from the kneeling position to run over and hug him. I stumbled in the process. Myles caught me before I hit the floor. He scooped me up and carried me to the couch.

"Wait here," Myles said and ran over to his luggage that was still by the door. He rushed back with his laptop in his hand as if I were in my final moments of life. "Tell me your symptoms." He pounded away at the keys.

Michael laughed at how Myles tried to diagnose me with the help of WebMD. His contagious laugh caused me to laugh. "Shh." I lifted my index finger to my puckered lips to hush my brother.

"I'm sorry if I'm being loud, Eva, but please tell me your symptoms," Myles said, thinking I was talking to him.

It was challenging to contain my laughter. Michael had jumped from the TV and back into my head.

"Eva," Myles hollered and waved his hand in my face.

I felt sadness for him and panic for myself. I didn't answer. If the website was accurate, it would expose the other side of me.

"Eva," Myles slowly called through clenched teeth. "Your symptoms," he said, clearly frustrated.

"Comply," Michael instructed.

At what seemed like twenty miles per minute, I listed each symptom. "It's weird, Myles. Sometimes I'm restless and tired at the same time. My head won't stop hurting. I haven't really been eating either." I wasn't sure what prompted me to laugh, but I did.

"When was the last time you ate?" Myles asked.

I thought about it before answering. I couldn't recall the last time I had anything to eat or drink. "I don't know," I replied.

Myles lowered his head and voice. "When was the last time you showered?"

I pushed his shoulder. "That's a rude thing to ask." No woman wanted to hear a man, *her* man, question her hygiene. But I did give it some thought. I knew I hadn't showered in a few days. How many exactly? I was unsure.

"I didn't mean to offend you, Eva."

"Well, you did, Myles."

He typed some more and said, "According to this, you have cancer. Get up so I can take you to the emergency room."

Michael laughed. *"Dummy."* I laughed too.

"This is no laughing matter, Eva. It may not be cancer, but you need to get checked out. I've never seen you like this."

"I'm fine," I said and tried to stand from the couch. I was too weak and sat back down.

"You are not fine. At least let me run you a hot bath and make you something to eat."

Again? The nerve of him. "Just leave me alone." I pulled the fuzzy gray blanket that Myles had covered me with over my face. I needed him to take the hint and disappear on his own before I helped him faster than Michael had planned.

Neither of the two men in my life understood my need for alone time. Myles continued playing doctor, and Michael continued talking. It was too much at one time, and I lost it. Unfortunately,

Myles was the one I lost it on. He had been in my face with the back of his hand pressed against my forehead, checking for a fever.

Michael talked loud and fast in my head as if he were an auctioneer, still ranting, *"Trick him, destroy him. Trick him, destroy him. Hurry up. Do it."*

"Move." I pushed Myles's hand from my face and jumped up from the couch. I didn't know where that energy came from. I stood in the middle of the floor with my palms cupped over my ears, spinning in circles. "Shut up, Michael. Please give me a break."

I remember the force when Michael grabbed my hand and used it as a weapon against Myles. My brother made me slap my boyfriend. I wasn't sure if it hurt him, but it certainly scared him enough to make him back away.

After my meltdown, the extra energy disappeared. Sweat poured from every inch of my flesh. Unsure of how I ended up seated Indian style on the floor, I exhausted what little was left in me by attempting to stand. My knees buckled, and the floor caught my bottom, and my eyes caught a glimpse of Myles, who was tucked away in the corner. He shook worse than an off-balance washing machine.

My mind flooded with questions. Was Michael messing with Myles too? Was I no longer the liaison? Was he not happy with my work? Or maybe Michael was in Myles's head trying to get him to do things to me. Nah. My brother wouldn't do that.

Those butterflies were back. They, too, were different. The flutter was no longer graceful but now painful.

"Myles," my voice cracked.

He didn't answer. He must have hated me. I didn't blame him.

I pulled my knees closer into my chest and buried my head in between them. If only I could have pulled them in even more to crush the rest of my soul, then I wouldn't have had to face what had taken place.

I didn't know how long we sat in opposite corners before the smell of Myles's cologne reached my nose. "Eva," he delicately said. "I'm here for you, but I need to understand what just happened." He wrapped his arms around me, and I immediately felt safe, even though my secret was out. Myles still loved me despite what he had just witnessed. However, what he did next made me question that thought.

Entry 11

Dear Diary:

"Let me get you some water," Myles said and vanished into the kitchen.

Once the ice cubes stopped pounding against the glass, I heard him speaking on the phone. Although only half of a wall divided the living room and kitchen, I couldn't make out what he said. I assumed it was his job, given how often they called and with no regard to time.

Myles ended the call before returning to my side with the water.

Both of my hands clutched the glass. I could feel my heartbeat returning to its usual harmonious thump as I took slow sips. Still, I couldn't bring myself to say anything nor make eye contact with Myles.

Worry invaded every inch of my brain. I wondered what Myles thought of me. Did he think I was some kind of freak? Then again, maybe he played it safe, fearing I'd do something to him. I wouldn't. I promised. That slap was a one-time thing, forced by Michael.

I tried to control my shaking hands, but the sudden ripples throughout the water caused a little spillage. Myles noticed. He crawled over to me and wrapped his arms around me again. I quickly drifted off into a relaxed, peaceful place, knowing that he still cared about me.

When the doorbell sounded, I sat up, perplexed. One of the perks of living on the fifth floor of the upscale Cambridge Lofts was the difficulty accessing the building. If anyone failed to check in at the reception desk and obtain a visitor's pass, they wouldn't get very far. Security was tight and posted throughout the building. A visitor's pass wasn't the only thing needed. The staff at the front desk also had to notify us. I was confused because the doorbell rang but we hadn't been informed.

"Who could that be?" I asked Myles.

Myles's look said he already knew who it was. When he opened the door, my eyes zoomed from the police badge to the baton and gun, and then quickly scanned the bulletproof vest.

Conversation came from the two-way radio, but I yelled over it. "How dare you, Myles?"

"Ma'am," the male officer said as a warning.

Myles hung his head. "I'm sorry, Eva."

"'I'm sorry, Eva,'" I repeated, mocking him. "You are not sorry. Is this your way of getting rid of me? You called the police to have me locked up. Is this your definition of love? Because I would have never done anything like this to you," I screamed at the top of my lungs, and I could feel my tonsils vibrate.

The female officer inched toward me. "Ma'am, you need to calm down."

Feeling brave and challenged, I took two steps toward her. I wasn't sure if she placed her hand on her gun or Taser, but it was enough to make Myles jump in front of me. Good thing he did, because I was not about to let them take me anywhere without a fight.

The sight of Myles pissed me off. And because he was so close to me, pretending like he cared and acting like he worked for the police department, trying to diffuse the situation, I felt the sudden urge to connect my flesh with his. *"Slap him,"* echoed throughout my ears. Although I promised never to do it again, I did. Every nerve in my body stung until I satisfied the craving. I felt powerful with each quick open-handed slap to his left cheek.

The officers dropped me. Pieces of the tan shag rug made their way into my mouth. I struggled to break free, but they kneeled on various parts of my body and cuffed me.

"Myles! Myles, please help me," I begged. "How could you do this to me? Please don't let them take me."

He mumbled those same stupid words. "I'm sorry, Eva."

"I hate you, Myles."

As I refused to walk, the female officer and three other male officers picked me up and escorted me to my awaiting chariot—the police cruiser. Once inside, I tried to kick the window out with my bare feet.

Frustrated with my actions, one of the male officers snatched the car door open and threatened to tase me if I didn't calm down. "Don't tase me. Shoot me. I dare you," I challenged him.

He pointed his gloved finger in my face. "I'm warning you," he said and slammed the door.

If I had a choice of death, jail, or the psych ward, death would be my first pick. I hated the admissions process, and my disdain grew worse each time. With every visit, everything was taken away from me. Simple things like belts and shoestrings were considered weapons. Why would they care if I chose to hang myself with them? My freedom was already gone. So was my privacy.

The hospital staff controlled my day-to-day activities, and my input didn't matter. We had to be awake at a particular hour. We were forced to take our meds and participate in individual and group activities whether we wanted to or not. I hated feeling the need to peek over my shoulder every second, not knowing when one of the crazies would harm me. Worst of all, I hated enduring the unidentifiable stenches floating past my nose in all directions.

This particular time, I chose death.

"Shoot me," I yelled as loud as I could to make sure they heard me through the glass. My request went ignored. The glass windows of the cruiser couldn't have been thick enough to drown out the sounds of my death wish.

The officers were locked in on whatever Myles said. His mouth hastily moved, and I was sure whatever came out was lies.

I believed they had conspired against me. They planned to torture me and dump my body into a wooded area. I accepted my life ending. I wanted that for myself until Michael showed up. *"Revenge. It's a part of the plan."*

I squirmed in the back of the squad car, trying to break free from the tightly locked cuffs. "Michael, please don't let them do this to me." I rocked back and forth. "I don't like this plan. I don't like this plan. I don't like this plan," I repeated and started banging my head against the window.

Multiple officers approached the car like they were ready to fight me. One opened the driver's side door and let all four windows down. "Ma'am, stop doing that."

I pleaded with my brother. "Michael, please do something. Can we change the plan? I don't want to go to jail, and I don't want to go to the hospital." His lack of response made me angry. "Michael, say something," I screamed.

"Eva, stop it! Michael is dead." Myles turned his back toward me, but that didn't stop me from hearing his sobs.

"That's what you think," I said.

The female officer rubbed his shoulder, trying to console him. "Stop touching him, you slut," I yelled and tried to wiggle out of the cuffs like I was a magician.

"Eva, please stop," Myles begged.

My throat burned from the constant yelling, and it continued to burn as I yelled, "You just want to get rid of me to be with your little slut over there."

"Who is Michael?" the female slut asked Myles.

He began to tell the most ridiculous story. "Michael was her brother—"

"*Is* my brother. You tried to kill him."

Myles held his hand up. "I can explain," he said. "Her brother and I were involved in a car accident years ago. He . . . died," Myles hesitantly said.

"He should be in jail, Officers. He tried to kill my brother. He's not dead. Michael, tell them you're not dead."

Michael was silent once again.

"Don't be shy. If you talk to them like you talk to me, they'll see and let me go."

Still nothing. I wondered why my brother chose to disappear at such an inopportune time.

Officers kept me in the back of the police car until the ambulance arrived. There was more resis-

tance on my behalf and a slight struggle. As soon
as they removed one of my wrists from the cuffs
to transition me to the ambulance, I broke free. I
hadn't run like that since making the decision to
step away from the track team. Wind blew through
my wild hair. It felt good.

"You can't catch me," I said and circled the
cruiser, laughing.

The officers surrounded the car but kept their
distance. "Ma'am, please don't make us tase you."

I stuck my tongue out. "Bet you won't shoot me."

"Eva, stop," Myles pleaded with me while walking toward me.

"If you come near me, I will slap you again."

I felt the jolt from the Taser. After that, I don't
remember much more. I woke up cuffed to a hospital bed, feeling sluggish and sick, similar to how
people described a hangover.

When I noticed the bracelets, a bit of adrenaline
kicked in. "Nurse! Nurse!" I wiggled and yelled.
Instead of the nurse coming, an officer stepped
into the room. It wasn't one from the house. A
different one. A mean one.

"Pipe down, ma'am. All that noise is not necessary." His hand rested on his gun like he was prepared to draw and shoot at any minute. Although I
didn't mind dying, I didn't understand his reaction.
I was sick, not a villain. Why so eager to shoot?
I was a buck fifty. He was over six feet tall and
muscular. He could take me with no problem.

"Can you uncuff me?" I gently asked. "My wrists are sore."

"That's your problem," he said and returned to his seat in the hallway.

After I was hydrated, patched up from a few minor cuts, and my vitals returned to normal, I was transferred to the psychiatric unit. For the next seventy-two hours, I wanted to hurt Myles more than Michael did.

Entry 12

Dear Diary:

Myles betrayed me. Much to my chagrin, he was waiting for me when I rounded the discharge station. He stood with his hands stuffed in the pockets of his black sweats. When we locked eyes, a slight grin lifted one of his chiseled cheekbones. Three days ago, he learned I was certified crazy, yet he was here instead of Uncle Bobby and Clara. I instantly froze, and every organ seemed to have uncomfortably traded places with another. Had something happened to my aunt and uncle? Did Myles have a suicide note from them?

I crept toward him. Instead of a greeting, I bombarded him with questions. "Where are Uncle Bobby and Clara? Are they okay? Do they know I'm here? Did something happen to them?"

Myles reached for me, but I turned my body so that no part of him brushed up against me. I wanted to claw his eyes out like I was a cat, but had I done that, the staff would have guided me right back to my room. I didn't want to leave with him, but I also didn't want to stay at the hospital.

When we got outside, he tried to hold my hand. Once again, I jerked away. "Don't touch me, back-stabber."

"I'm sorry you feel that way, Eva. I had to make sure you got help."

I scoffed at how casually the word "help" rolled off his tongue. "You were not trying to help me. What you did was embarrass me."

Myles reached into the car and pulled out a bouquet of flowers. Normally, that gesture would have put a smile on my face, but I just didn't like him or any attempt he made to downplay what he had done.

"You can just drop me off in Augusta or as close to it as possible," I demanded. If it had not been for the rain, fierce winds, and lightning strikes, I would have taken my chances and walked the seventy miles to Uncle Bobby and Clara's.

Even though I told Myles not to touch me, he didn't listen. He eased his hand up to my face and stroked my cheek with his thumb. My mind reeled. Should I turn around and check myself back into the hospital or unleash my wrath on him?

"I said don't touch me," I said, sternly issuing a warning shot.

Myles held his hands up like he was being robbed. "Okay."

"Are you going to take me to Augusta? Or do I need to call for a ride?"

"I am not taking you anywhere except for home," Myles replied. "Our home."

"No, that's your home, and I don't want to go there with you."

"Fair enough. But it's our home, and I would like for us to go there together, but I will respect your wishes if you'd rather go somewhere else to cool off." He paused, took a breath, and inched his hand to my face again, forcing me to look at him. He added, "I hope that you'll come *home* so we can figure things out. Together."

I hid a blush. I was taken aback that he hadn't given up on me. Unlike my blood relatives, not once had Myles said one derogatory thing about me, and he was in the midst of it all. Had this been my family, they would have hurled a million insults my way as soon as they laid eyes on me. Well, not Uncle Bobby or Clara. They had more patience than Job. I always wondered if they thought things and just didn't say them. They couldn't have. Not with how much they defended me.

Myles had a point. The loft was practically my home since I'd slowly moved a lot of my things in and hadn't slept at Uncle Bobby and Clara's since. While my name wasn't on anything, he made me feel like what he had was mine.

There was something about standing in the middle of a thunderstorm, reevaluating life, and weighing my options.

Where I lived with Myles provided more excitement than with my aunt and uncle. Not to mention, it was safer. I was sure when Uncle Bobby and Clara purchased their two-story family home many years ago, it wasn't surrounded by liquor stores on every corner or infested with crime. But I questioned how the loft neighbors would look at me after the show I put on. And I wondered how they looked at Myles and why he even asked me back.

Living on the lake was good for my soul, though. The colors seemed brighter, and the air smelled fresher. The atmosphere no longer reeked of gasoline and gun powder residue. Bakeries and coffee houses lined every corner near the lake and were pleasing with every inhale. I gladly traded in being awakened each morning at five a.m. by a loud train for a distant alarm clock when Myles got ready for his day. Plus, it beat sleeping in the back bedroom that faced an overgrown lot.

With Myles, from the moment I opened my eyes, my bare feet tapped across the hardwood floors to my favorite seat in the house by the window. As people strolled by, I often created scenarios in my mind of what I felt their life was like. Sometimes I made them have problems similar to mine so I wouldn't feel so alone.

The scenery at the lofts and what it did to my spirit determined my final decision. I didn't tell Myles. I opened the door and sat inside.

The car was mostly quiet other than occasional small talk on Myles's part. He flipped through radio stations before finally powering the radio down. He sighed before asking, "Do you want to talk?"

I would have much rather listened to the squeakiness from the windshield wipers clearing away the heavy rain than listen to Myles. "No," I replied with a sigh to match his.

My response must have flown over his head, because he kept asking questions anyway.

"Is there anything I can do to make you feel better?" he asked.

"No. You've done enough, so please stop talking to me." Even though I had planned to return home with Myles, he still needed to pay for what he did, at least until I felt he was sorry.

Myles still didn't get it. "I understand you're not happy with the decision I made, but I did what I felt was best."

"Best for who, Myles? For you? You probably had a girl there while I was locked away."

"Man, why would I bring a girl to our house? You act like you're the only one affected by what happened."

"When we get home, you'd better believe I'm going to check the visitor's log. I swear if you had another girl there . . ." I didn't bother to finish the threat because I didn't know how he would react.

"You're crazy." Myles and I both gasped. That had been the first negative, irresponsible thing he'd let slip. "Eva, I promise I didn't mean . . ." His voice trailed off.

From the moment I saw Myles waiting for me, my gut told me it wouldn't be long before something bad happened. My left knuckle stung, and the side of Myles's cheek instantly discolored. He brought this upon himself. "Don't ever call me crazy. Hurry up and get me home."

Myles accelerated. The roar from the Hemi engine drowned out my heartbeat, which thumped in my ears from anger. We whisked through several two-lane roads like we were in a drag-racing competition even though the posted speed limit was thirty-five. I glanced at the speedometer and noticed the speed climbing. We had reached eighty-five miles per hour before I spoke up.

"What is wrong with you?" I asked. "You have no right to be upset."

He clenched his jaw. "I'm trying to hurry up and get you home like you said."

"Slow this car down, smart-ass."

It was like I was talking to myself, because he accelerated even more.

"Is this what you did to Michael? Is this how you tried to kill my brother?" Just as quickly as I reminded Myles of Michael, I suddenly had a death wish of my own. I unfastened my seat belt with my left hand, leaned over, and grabbed the steering wheel with my right. "I wish I were dead, and you deserve to be too."

We struggled over control of the wheel. Myles fought to keep us on the road while I fought to run us off. Because he was stronger than me, I needed to loosen his grip. I bit his hand. It wasn't an ordinary bite. I channeled a pit bull. I latched on and sank my teeth into his flesh while I shook my head and growled.

Instead of him reacting the way I wanted him to, tires screeched as we slid along the wet pavement and came to a complete stop.

"Why did you do that?" I shouted.

Myles remained calm as blood oozed from his wound. Other than the wipers and seat belt warning, nothing. I wanted to bite him again to make him talk.

"I know you hear me talking to you, Myles."

Finally, he mumbled, "Despite what you think, I did not intentionally hurt Michael."

"I beg to differ, but that's not what I'm talking about. I was expecting you to slam on the brakes and send me flying through the windshield like you did to my brother."

"Car manufacturers install safety features for a reason. That annoying dinging you hear alerts me that someone doesn't have on a seat belt. I have mine on," Myles sarcastically said while tugging at the strap. "Just like I didn't intentionally hurt Michael, I would never intentionally hurt you. I thought I had proven that to you, or at least was working toward that."

"Whatever." I rested my head against the headrest and folded my arms across my chest.

Myles sat for a while, looking zoned out, before he merged back into traffic. With all my adrenaline gone and the lack of rest from the hospital, I was exhausted. I let my seat back as far as it would go and slept the rest of the drive. I woke up to Uncle Bobby and Clara standing on their front porch, waiting to welcome me back.

Entry 13

Dear Diary:

I could not believe Myles had dropped me off on the curb of Uncle Bobby and Clara's like I was trash. He didn't even warn me. In fact, he had no words for me at all. But he did have plenty for my aunt and uncle.

"Oh, dear, what happened to your hand? You're bleeding." Clara frantically hurried to Myles to survey the damage I caused.

He tossed a devilish look in my direction but didn't verbally snitch. "It's nothing," he coolly responded.

"I'll get the first aid kit," Clara said and disappeared into the house.

"Hey, Unc. How's it going?" Myles greeted my uncle and took a seat on the porch.

Uncle Bobby stopped rocking to respond. "Good, son. Nasty injury you have there."

"It's nothing."

"Looks like something to me," Uncle Bobby countered.

Clara busted through the door with a kit in her hand and tended to Myles.

I felt offended. They were supposed to be on my side. If I was mad at Myles, they should've been mad too, not giving him familial titles and tending to wounds he clearly deserved.

"I'm dropping Eva off. I'll reach out to you to arrange a time to drop off her things," he said once Clara finished patching him up.

"Sounds good. I can come and pick them up if needed," Uncle Bobby offered. It was like he had expected me and my things. No shock. No questions. Clara too. But when did Myles have time to discuss any of that with them? Maybe they had expected me to ruin the relationship and weren't surprised to see me returning to impose on their lives once again.

"Thank you, sir. I'll let you know." Myles shook Uncle Bobby's hand, thanked Clara, and returned to his car.

He didn't say one word to me. I didn't care to be around him anymore anyway, but at least he could've wished me a good life before he peeled out.

"Come on, dear," Clara sighed. "I made you a sandwich."

I frowned. "How did you know I was coming?"

"Myles called."

It clicked. I remembered falling asleep in the car.

Uncle Bobby grabbed my wrist, stopping me from entering the house. "That was a nasty injury." He let go of my wrist, then quickly glanced at me and then back to the street. I wasn't sure if Myles told, but Uncle Bobby knew I caused it.

Weeks passed as I kind of involuntarily resumed being a full-time resident of my old dwelling. Myles had returned my things like he said he would. I was asleep when he came, and then I cried like a mourner, knowing he followed through with kicking me out without trying to win me back. Myles had given up on me, and there was nothing I could do about it.

There were good days and lousy ones dealing with my first-ever breakup, but luckily there were no more hospitalizations. The unidentifiable whispers were gone. Michael too. Although I took my medication as prescribed and responded fairly decently to treatment, I still rated life on the blah scale. The suicidal thoughts would come and go, but I didn't have a plan to harm myself. The trust that I had built with Clara allowed me the comfort of going to her when I felt off. She would help me readjust my thinking and soothe me back into a safe place.

I talked a good game, but I missed Myles. I missed everything about him: his expensive scent, his braying laughter, the way his eyes showed me that I had his full attention whenever he looked at me. The way he looked at me. That was the best feeling. I'd often catch him stealing glances. Pure love visible. And I ruined it.

I wanted to cry to Clara, but I needed to be woman enough to clean up the mess I had made. I took a chance and called Myles. Better to live with rejection than what-ifs.

To my surprise, Myles answered. "You okay?"

"I'll do anything to make this right, Myles."

"You sure about that?" he countered.

"I promise."

"Hold on," he said, and then a lingering silence followed. I thought he had hung up, but when I looked at my phone to verify, the timer still rolled.

"Eva, you still there?" He finally returned about three minutes later.

"I'm here," desperately rushed from my mouth.

"I'll be there to pick you up Thursday around"— Myles paused, and I heard him shuffle through papers—"twelve fifteen," he said. "Be ready."

"Where are we going? And how should I dress?"

"Dress however. No questions. You'll see when we get there."

Myles arrived at precisely twelve fifteen like he said he would. He didn't get out and do his gentleman thing by opening the car door for me like he usually would. He let his window down and yelled to my aunt and uncle, who stood on the porch watching me leave like they were watching their child board the bus for her first day of kindergarten.

"Good morning," I greeted him with a smile.

Myles didn't look my way as he returned the greeting. "Good morning. How was your night?"

"Pretty quiet, and yours?"

"Same."

Time away from me seemed to have changed him. He was distant, which confused me because he had invited me out. Made me wonder if Myles had a hint of mental illness himself.

As I studied Myles's body language, I noticed his dressed-down attire compared to mine. He wore a sweatsuit while I dressed for a more exciting occasion. "Should I run back in and change?" I asked. "I have on a dress, and you have on sweats."

"What you have on is fine."

I wondered when he had noticed since he'd refused to look in my direction.

When we arrived at our destination, I snatched off my seat belt and looked around. Myles was pretty romantic, and when he told me to be ready, I assumed he had planned to whisk me away for some fun to make up for having me committed. Judging by the row of office buildings, I wasn't sure what he had up his sleeve, but I unbuckled my seat belt, ready to make amends.

"Gastroenterologist, dermatology, endocrinology," I read off the signs.

My heart raced as I sucked in as much air as my lungs could hold. With the numerous suites of offices in buildings aligned side by side, there were more possibilities than the last sign I had read. *He wouldn't.* Rather than overreact, I decided on a different approach.

"Myles, is there something wrong with you?" My mind became flooded with harrowing ideas. Maybe his health was declining, and he didn't know how to tell me, so he brought me to the doctor with him. Myles needed me for emotional support. This wasn't what it looked like.

"This visit isn't for me," he said matter-of-factly.

"It's not for me either," I sassed.

Apparently, it was what it looked like, and from the looks of it, Myles had driven me to a psychiatrist.

"Eva, please. This is for your benefit."

I fastened my seat belt. "I'm not getting out."

"That's fine. If you don't want to get out, you don't have to. It's your choice," Myles said.

"You're right." I patted my chest and added, "It's my choice. You should've asked me first. Why would you think this was okay?"

"This is the aftercare follow-up appointment the hospital scheduled for you. With you being back at your aunt and uncle's, it got overlooked. When you called, I called them to reschedule it."

"Well, I'm not doing it. I thought you were taking me somewhere to apologize for calling the police on me."

Myles shook his head. "I did what was right."

"Calling the police on me was not right. Bringing me to a psychiatrist without my permission is not right."

"I just want you to be okay, Eva. After everything that has happened, I am trying to get you some help. Can you please give it a chance?" Myles grabbed my hand, but I snatched it away.

"Are you bringing me here to have me recommitted so you can run around with some other girl? It's that officer, isn't it?" I won't lie. She was beautiful. Fit, chocolate, and her makeup was flawless. I bet as a cop, she had her life together. She knew how to protect and serve, while all I knew how to do was cause a ruckus.

The back of Myles's head bobbed against the headrest. "There is no other girl. That officer came to do her job, that's it. I don't even know what her name is. Now, can we please go inside?"

I wasn't convinced Myles told the truth. There had to be another woman. One who treated him better than I ever could. And one who gave him sex. "Who is she? Is she in there?" I pointed in the direction of the building. "You want her to make fun of me?"

Myles closed his eyes. Through clenched teeth, he said, "There is no 'she.' I am not trying to get rid of you. If I were, then I wouldn't be here. Despite everything, I don't want to get rid of you. I want you to get the necessary help so that we can move on in a stable capacity."

"I am stable."

Myles waved around his scarred hand. "You said you'd do anything. This is anything. The choice is yours. Either you get help, or there is no chance of us rekindling our flame."

"You can't give me an ultimatum."

"And we can't continue on this path." This time, Myles drew a circle around the healed bite mark. I really did a number on him. I could still see the teeth marks.

Stubbornness ran deep within the Moss blood. I would not fold over an empty threat. All it did was fuel the resistance even more. "You must be the crazy one if you think I'm worried about you leaving me. If you wanna leave, then bye." Days ago, I had cried. But the mere thought of Myles threatening me instantly made me defensive.

"Eva, please," Myles pleaded.

"I've already told you, Michael, I am not going inside." I bit down on my pinky finger knuckle once I realized what I had said. "I'm sorry. I meant Myles."

"This is exactly why we need to go inside. I choose you and would love to see a future between us." His finger hovered over the ignition button. "But I can't make you."

Outside of Uncle Bobby and Clara, no one had ever chosen me. I thought I would easily jump in, do as Michael instructed, and continue with my life, but there was something inexplicable about Myles Sanders that tugged at my heartstrings and mesmerized me. Not a single soul would understand what went on inside my mind. Honestly, I didn't understand it, but Myles wanted to understand and help me. I just needed to be courageous enough to face Michael. He would realize that I'd finally fallen in love, and one day he'd approve of the budding relationship.

Entry 14

Dear Diary:

The people in the clinic were nothing like me. In fact, they were beyond crazy. Compared to what my eyes viewed, I was perfect. Perhaps the sanity of whoever scheduled me for a visit needed to be checked instead of mine.

I watched as a man sat in the corner talking to himself. Well, I couldn't say he wasn't among company, but I didn't see anyone else. Three rows up and two chairs over sat an interracial couple who were all over each other. This place was a one-stop shop—pills and porn.

"Here." Myles stepped to my side and attempted to pass me a pen.

I turned my nose up. "What do you want me to do with that?"

"Sign in," he sarcastically responded.

Over my dead body. There was no way I would touch that pen. Judging by the patients in the lobby, there was no telling where their hands had been. "No, thank you." I took a step back, creating more distance between me and the sign-in sheet.

"Eva Moss has a one o'clock appointment," Myles said to the receptionist as he signed me in himself.

The receptionist gave a welcome spiel and handed Myles a clipboard with paperwork attached to it. A thick stack at that.

Myles completed most of the paperwork before I leaned over and asked, "Is this appointment for me or you?"

Just as I was about to make another sarcastic comment, a guy who was clearly confused on the seasons sat in the empty chair beside me, sandwiching me in.

"Hey there, cutie patootie. Can I get your number?" he asked.

I stared at his multicolored wool beanie, and my eyes traced over his heavily scarred forehead and down to his glasses. One side was missing a temple, and the glasses themselves were united by a wad of dirty tape.

I didn't respond because I assumed Myles, *my boyfriend,* would speak up and honor me. He had his head buried in paperwork and said nothing. I thought that if I remained quiet, the stranger would take the hint and go away. Instead, he waved his red-stained hands near my face and repeated the question.

My eyes followed his hands when they rested on the knees of his worn khaki pants. I wondered if his hands were discolored from food or blood from a murder that he'd committed.

I nervously stammered over my words, automatically thinking the worst of the stranger. "I . . . I . . . I'm with him. He . . . he's my boyfriend." I pointed to Myles, who pretended to be oblivious to the harassment.

"Excuse me, sir," the guy addressed Myles. "Can I have your girlfriend's phone number?" His eyes remained locked on Myles even though he continued to lean forward. He had on a pair of black flip-flops and had started scratching his big toe that was covered in scabs.

Myles chuckled as he got up from his seat to return the paperwork. I followed him. I would even touch a pen if that meant getting away from the weirdo. More so, the clinic in general.

Time lingered. An hour or so passed, and we were still waiting. Myles was preoccupied with answering emails on his phone. It was a different story for me. I repositioned myself in my chair several times while taking in the poor ambiance. The office I had visited before looked like top interior designers had decorated it compared to this one. Paint peeled from the walls and rested on the old, stained carpet. The fake leather sitting chairs were in dire need of being replaced, and the baseboards looked like they had been accumulating dirt for quite some time.

I tapped Myles on the shoulder. "You couldn't have taken me to a better facility?"

"The hospital set this up," he replied without lifting his head from his phone.

"But as much money as you make, you couldn't find me anything better?"

Myles decided to give me another ultimatum. "Another facility may be a possibility depending on how serious you are with getting the help you need."

I heard wheezing and felt hot cinnamon breath against my neck. I slowly rolled my head in the direction of the other chair. I had forgotten about the weirdo. He was in our conversation like we were talking to him and we had known him forever.

"Can I help you?" I asked with an attitude.

"I was trying to see if I can get your number."

I inhaled, prepared to dig into him, but I was interrupted.

"Moss."

I ran to the young lady as if my life depended on it. Myles was hot on my heels as she escorted us to the doctor's office.

"Dr. Monroe," the petite man introduced himself and extended his hand for a shake.

Myles returned the gesture. "I'm Myles Sanders, and this is Eva Moss."

Although this wasn't my first rodeo to a psychiatrist's office, I was nervous. I held on to Myles's waist for protection even though he was the reason for the visit.

"We have a shy one," Dr. Monroe said. "I don't bite."

He could've fooled me. His lips hid behind a thick mustache long overdue for a trim. The tips curled up much like the *Monopoly* man. My eyes cased him and his office. Because of his height, I imagined his feet swung in the oversized leather chair that still spun behind the large cedar desk that took up most of the office space. The desk was littered with paper. Mounted on the wall behind him was a leaflet display that housed brochures covering various mental health illnesses. His degree hung next to that—class of 1979. I wasn't even born yet. His frail voice notified me that he was ready to begin the assessment.

Myles did most of the talking because I wouldn't. Everything Myles said, Dr. Monroe jotted down the old-fashioned way, which I didn't understand because a Dell monitor was alive on his desk. Then I remembered he graduated in 1979.

My primary interaction was a shoulder shrug here and there.

Finally, Dr. Monroe laid his pencil down and placed one hand on top of the other. "Ms. Moss, I understand you were previously diagnosed with depression, but I am afraid that is no longer the case."

Myles cocked his head to the side, confused. "I'm sorry. I don't understand."

"All her behavior patterns over the years align with bipolar disorder with psychotic features."

"I don't know much about mental illness, but how could her diagnosis change like that and that fast?" Myles asked, still looking confused. "Did the hospital misdiagnose her?"

Dr. Monroe reached behind him and retrieved a brochure on bipolar disorder. He highlighted vital details as he read the symptoms aloud. "Not necessarily. As you get older, untreated bipolar symptoms tend to intensify. Maybe you've noticed shifts in your mood, hallucinations, sometimes a difference in your speech, and even reckless behavior."

Myles nodded his head to everything Dr. Monroe said.

"There also tend to be episodes of extreme paranoia in the mix as well. Those are all signs," Dr. Monroe continued.

I didn't like it, especially because he said these things in front of Myles. "And you determined this how?" I crossed my arms over my chest, demanding an explanation. One that I could debunk. He may have had credentials, but he had no idea what he was talking about. That diagnosis was way too fast, and I never parted my lips to speak.

"Well, there were several factors that led me to this diagnosis. I also reviewed all the notes from your previous hospital admissions, dating back to the very first one, as well as the notes from your current provider at Augusta Behavioral Health."

Myles's body jerked forward. "Previous hospitalizations and current provider?"

It felt like someone had sucked all the air from the room. Even the ticking from the cuckoo clock that hung on Dr. Monroe's wall seemed to stop. What a befitting clock to have in a place like this. I had never gotten around to mentioning to Myles those facts that Dr. Monroe spilled.

"I'm sorry, Doctor," Myles said and turned to me. 'You've been through this process before?"

"Something like that."

"And you never bothered to tell me?"

"It wasn't your business."

Myles groaned, visibly upset. "It's my business if I'm involved with you. Here I am thinking this is the first time, but you've dealt with this all along."

Dr. Monroe interjected, "I know this can be overwhelming, not only for the patient but for the family as well. There are many things to factor in. I've found that clients respond better to treatment when they have support. It's not easy admitting a mental health diagnosis. There's backlash and judgment for the patient and embarrassment for the families because they face the same ridicule. Many people don't take the time to understand mental illness. It doesn't always have to be viewed negatively. The good news is, with your help, Mr.

Sanders, along with the right combination of medication, including an injection and consistent therapy, Eva can live a very normal and satisfying life."

I was all in with Dr. Monroe until the end. "Wait. What do you mean by an injection and consistent therapy? I see a psychiatrist once every two months. That's enough therapy for me. And there is no way I will let anyone in this nasty clinic stick me with anything." I looked, squirmed, and scratched my arm.

"The psychiatrist manages your meds. I want to get you in with a licensed therapist who can provide coping techniques and a listening ear in between and support groups to do the same. Maybe even make a few friends who can relate to what you're going through."

I shook my head in disapproval. "Support groups? You mean me and a bunch of people in a room together?"

Dr. Monroe nodded. "Think about it," he said. "I am prescribing you with five hundred milligrams of Depakote. I want you to take one in the morning and two at night. This will help to stabilize your mood." Dr. Monroe talked and scribbled on a prescription pad in front of him. It was so much information, and he wasn't finished. "Please consider the injection that I mentioned." He paused to retrieve another brochure on Abilify Maintena.

"You will need to get these shots once a month, but they will be extremely beneficial to you, Ms. Moss."

"I have a question," I said.

"Ask away."

"Do you take the injection?"

"I don't."

"So how can you tell me it will work for me if you have never taken it?"

"Eva," Myles said and then apologized to the doctor.

"I've studied mental health for a long time. I stand by everything I recommend. Just try it out and see how it works for you. If you feel it's not successful, we can always try something else. Again, I'm confident that everything I've recommended will do wonders for you. You won't have to exclude yourself when it comes to doing normal things. Trust me, please."

"Normal" floated around in my head. I had always wanted to be that. It wouldn't hurt to try. "I'll give it a try. Only the injection and medication." The support groups may have been helpful if I were looking for support, but sitting in a roomful of strangers and hearing about their issues would have been a setback for me. I needed to rid myself of my problems, not take on more. *"Normal"* was enticing. I just hoped Michael wouldn't be too upset.

Dr. Monroe concluded our session. "I'll have the nurse draw up the injection. Give it a few days. You'll see a major difference. Follow up with me in a month."

Entry 15

Dear Diary:
Despite my skepticism, Dr. Monroe was right. The changes were gradual but noticeable day by day, as he said they would be. At my four-week follow-up appointment, not only did I show up twenty minutes early, but I signed myself in and apologized to the entire office staff for my poor behavior during my first visit.

First, I handed them a fruit basket that I picked up on the way to my appointment. "I am so sorry for the way I behaved during my first visit. I am ashamed. Know that I was raised better than that."

The front desk staff appreciated the gesture. One even gave me a pass. "It's okay. We understand bad days happen."

"Even so, I had no right to act the way that I did, and I just want to apologize again and thank you for your patience."

I wondered if I had finally reached normal status. Technically, I never knew what that felt like, but I knew I felt differently: smiles, energy, and overall joy compared to isolating myself and sleeping my life away. The jolt of confidence motivated me to begin journaling again. Every day, I started by writing the emotion I felt the moment I opened my eyes and then goals to ensure the day would sail along smoothly.

The excessive energy was amazing. The oomph taking over my once-sluggish body afforded me the drive to tackle my domestic responsibilities around the house. The positive changes to my mood allowed me to embrace my role as Myles's girlfriend.

The hands on the clock had finally taken a sixty-second rest where I needed them to be. Myles was due home at five p.m. He had no idea he'd walk in on a surprise from me. Things were not quite finished, but I hoped he would at least admire the effort.

I heard Myles at the front door as Luther Vandross belted out an extended note. I ran from the kitchen, checking on dinner, back to the fresh laundry strewn across the couch. I held a pair of Myles's boxers so he would see me folding them when he walked in. Michael always told me there was nothing sexier than a woman folding her man's drawers. As if he knew. That boy was close to graduating, and our mother still washed his clothes.

When I saw Myles out of the corner of my eye, I immediately said, "Laundry is done. It's just not folded. Sorry."

I turned around and noticed he was in awe.

"I wasn't sure in what order you wanted your shirts hung, so I grouped them by arm length. All your long-sleeved shirts are together, and . . ." I quit blabbing when his Cole Haans stopped tapping against the floor.

A proud smile parted his lips. "Wow."

I pointed to the kitchen. "Dinner is almost ready."

Those shoes started tapping again. This time they were headed directly toward me. He spun me around and squeezed me from behind. "You cooked, too?"

I nodded and mumbled, "Something like that." I had never cooked a real meal before. Easy stuff. Hot dogs, fried bologna sandwiches, and other small, effortless meals. My mother had always cooked for me, and then Clara became my cook. Luckily, I had found a magazine in the loft lobby with a good-looking recipe inside. Of the three twenty-minute meals, I chose the grilled chicken romesco, whatever that was.

Myles pulled my hair behind my ear, exposing the side of my face, and planted a lingering kiss on my cheek. "I love you."

And there were those words that Myles would yell to me when we were younger. We rode the same bus, and our stop was before his. He always made it a point to drop the window to yell, "I love you, Eva." Laughter would erupt from everyone on the bus while Michael sang, "Myles and Eva sitting in a tree, k-i-s-s-i-n-g," the remainder of the walk home. This time Myles meant it.

I never thought those words would come from a man who didn't share my DNA. Not seriously anyway. It was only fitting that I said it back. "I love you too, Myles Sanders."

We started rocking from side to side to the music. I instantly thought of Uncle Bobby and Clara. I'd finally gotten that moment, and it felt good. Myles huffed when the oven timer sounded.

"Dinner's ready," I announced, tapping Myles's forearm for him to loosen his grip. "Although you look handsome, you still have on your work clothes. Change while I set the table."

"Yes, ma'am." Myles disappeared into his room.

Smoke assaulted my nose and mouth when I opened the oven. How did I ruin dinner? How hard could it have been? I followed the directions closely, except for the time. Once the twenty minutes were up, the food didn't look like the picture, so I popped it back in the oven. It burned.

"Good as new," I mumbled once I scraped the charred parts off with a butter knife. Michael taught me that skill.

Myles was seated at the dining room table when I plated the food. "This all smells so good," he said. His smile quickly diminished when he looked at this plate. "Let's bless the food."

"As many meals as you and I have eaten together, you have never once suggested grace."

He cleared his throat and struggled to find words. "Nah . . ." He chuckled a bit. "It's just that, um, you know, you're making changes, and I feel like this would be a good addition to our relationship."

"Mm-hm."

He snickered and snorted. "You don't have to believe me."

"Don't worry, because I don't."

Myles reached across the table and stroked my hand. "Come on, beautiful, don't do me like that."

Since I felt cursed, I wasn't much of a believer anyway, but I was determined to hear what Myles would say. "It was your suggestion. Let's hear it." I bowed my head and listened to the saddest prayer I'd ever heard out of the mouth of an adult.

"God is great. God is good. Help us, Lord, eat this food."

One of my eyebrows arched. *This can't be real.* I peeped out of my left eye and watched him as he prayed the kindergarten prayer.

"Amen," we said in sync.

We both sat staring back and forth between each other and the dreadful-looking meal. Even though I scraped the charred marks off, it was still evident by Myles's inability to cut his chicken that I had overcooked it. The room sounded like a symphony starring our eating utensils and plates. Honestly, I was afraid to take a bite, so I knew Myles had to be too.

"Wanna order a pizza?" I asked.

Through hysterical laughter, Myles said, "Thought you'd never ask."

While he ordered the pizza and wings from the app on his phone, I laid out a blanket in front of the fireplace. Granted, it was summertime in Georgia, and the high for the day had spiked past a hundred. Even with the sun making its way home for the evening, it was still sweltering. However, the fire was the focal point in the magazine that I worked hard to mimic, and I had to see it through. I turned the air down as low as it would go in an attempt to balance out the heat.

"Sixty-five minutes on delivery," Myles informed me.

"Jeez. That long?"

"You can eat the chicken you made," he said and tried his best to hold in his laugh.

I rolled my eyes and remembered the fresh loaf of bread I had picked up from Artino's Bakery and Deli. Myles loved that place. I became fond of them after he took me there on a date. And since this was the first time I had planned a romantic evening, I decided to surprise him with a loaf.

"Wait here." I hopped up from the blanket like a kangaroo.

His eyes twinkled as soon as he spotted the Artino's custom black bread bag. "You didn't."

"I did," I responded.

We shared the bread and talked for the next hour before he said, "Thank you so much for doing this, babe. You have really outdone yourself."

The fire crackled as if it were underscoring my good deeds.

"Even though dinner wasn't edible?" I asked.

"Even though dinner wasn't edible," Myles agreed. "The fact that you went out of your way to do all this for me means a lot."

"I can't believe I expected us to eat that burnt chicken."

Myles had such a distinct laugh that also happened to be infectious. The laughter turned into intense stares. He always had a way of ogling me to the point where heat burned my cheeks. I had looked into his round brown eyes on many occasions but had never seen such lust.

Myles's tongue rolled across his thick lips. "I appreciate you. I'm sorry if I don't tell you enough. Or show you."

Either the heat-air balance was off, or something about Myles raised my inner temperature.

My back pressed against the floor from the weight of Myles climbing on top of me. "You know, I've never done this before," I whispered in his ear. "I'm scared, but I want to."

We were so caught up in the moment that it took the concierge multiple times to reach us.

"I love you." Myles pecked my forehead and raised himself off me. He started toward the door but turned to me. Innocence replaced lust. "This is actually perfect timing, babe. I told you I wanted to do things the right way."

"But I want to," I whined.

He shook his head. "I respect you and Michael too much to go that far without you having my last name," he said and twisted the deadbolt to the unlocked position.

My objections dissolved when I saw the pizza delivery guy looking back at me. He carried an uncanny resemblance to Michael. Mainly the dimples.

"Is it just me, or did that kid remind you of Michael?" I asked before the driver was out of sight.

Myles sighed. "Definitely. I'm glad I'm not alone with that thought."

I returned the sigh. "I miss my brother."

"I know you do. I miss him too. I'm sorry, Eva."

I smiled at him. "Stop apologizing. We are moving forward, right?" I shocked myself. For the first time, I excused Myles for what happened to Michael. No rage. No blame. Simply understanding and pardon.

I didn't know what the manufacturers put in my medication, but it worked wonders at overriding my sometimes-evil way of thinking. Plus, it felt good to talk about Michael.

Who would have thought that Eva Ann Moss could feel this amped about life?

Finally.

Entry 16

Dear Diary:

Life was good. Life was great. Treatment had been consistent and effective. I still made the chaise by the window my home each day, but instead of assigning flaws while people watching, I gave them all a happily ever after like I knew I would have.

"Babe," Myles said when he emerged from his room, interrupting me assigning a jogger the title of Olympic gold medalist. "Can you be dressed by two?"

"For what? Last time you told me to be ready by a certain time, you drove me to that clinic."

He gave me the best side-eye I'd ever seen from anyone, let alone a man. "Things are great between us, so there's no need for all that."

I nodded and took in the elderly couple strolling by and holding hands. "Look, Myles."

He peeked. "What am I looking at?"

I pointed, and my finger followed their stroll. "You see them? What story would you give them?"

"What do you mean?" he asked.

"If you had to assign them a life story, what would you say?"

He shrugged, obviously uninterested in my game. "I don't know. They're old and lived a long life."

"You are so boring. Jazz it up."

Myles stared at the couple. When he smiled, I just knew he had found them a beautiful love story. "That's his old side piece."

I rolled my eyes. "Really? You couldn't come up with anything better than that?"

"What? I'm a man. I don't think like that. This game is stupid anyway."

I returned my gaze to them. They were almost out of view. "Do you want to hear what I'd say?"

"Not really, but I know you're going to tell me anyway."

"Exactly. I'd say they're celebrating their fiftieth wedding anniversary, and she doesn't know it, but he's planning to propose again to her. Then he's going to whisk her away to a private island for a recommittal ceremony." In the stillness, I replaced the faces of that couple with the faces of Myles and me. "Cute, right?" My fantasy had vanished right along with the couple.

"I don't use words like cute," he responded.

"Yes, you do. You tell me I look cute all the time."

"Oh. Well, that's different," he laughed.

"One more." I grabbed his shirt to pull him back to the window. "Them. And don't say anything stupid. It has to be romantic."

He studied the young couple, holding hands, laughing. "She's his young side piece." His shoulders bounced from the laughter that ripped through his body.

I shook my head, ignoring his stupidity. "Here's what I think. They are newly in love and are discussing their future and the number of kids they will have. The guy says seven, but the girl says two and makes a joke about science advancing to make it possible for men to carry babies."

"I hope I'm dead when that happens," Myles said. "You are too into this watching of the people."

"It's called *people watching*. And yes, it is very entertaining." I returned my focus to the street while Myles fumbled around, doing whatever he did. I couldn't help but ask the question that burned in my mind ever since assigning the young couple a story. "Myles, do you want marriage and children?"

For whatever reason, Myles appeared nervous. I thought maybe it was because he had never intended to marry and didn't want to sell me a false dream. I understood. Things were good between us, but still he knew my dark secret, which was something impossible to pretend didn't exist.

"Wear sneakers. Ready by two," he reminded me and disappeared into his room.

When two o'clock arrived, I was ready and waiting with a pair of neon green Nikes that I had guiltily purchased with the credit card Myles had given me to splurge whenever I wanted.

"Where are we going?" I asked, already knowing he'd do the usual and not tell me.

"Taking a stroll around the lake," he surprisingly responded.

I slowed my stride, unsure if I wanted to go. "On a Sunday?"

"Yeah. What's wrong with that?" Myles walked ahead and called for the elevator.

"We usually go on Saturdays when the food trucks, entertainment, and crowds are there."

"And because of my heavy workload and travel, we've missed a few Saturdays. It's nice out, less crowded, and we can enjoy one another's company." He stepped into the elevator and held the door open for me. "You coming or not?"

Reluctantly, I joined him.

It was weird walking the lake. It was empty. Unlively. Usually, tents would be lined up, filled with vendors. Different styles of music would mix to create one unique sound. Granted, crowds increased my anxiety, but it was my therapist's idea for me to take steps toward overcoming my agoraphobia. Just like with Dr. Monroe, I thought she was the one who needed help when she first made the suggestion.

"Jump in and don't think about it," she had told me.

I threatened to fire her. These weren't swimming lessons. I couldn't jump in and dog-paddle my way around. However, I did, and I often used Myles as a shield around people. If anyone got closer than what I was comfortable with, I'd clutch a part of his body and tuck my face into the back of his armpit. Each time, he'd tell me, "Loosen up. I'm not going to let anyone hurt you." Eventually, I grew to trust him when he said that.

"Are they having something here today?" I asked Myles when I noticed quite a few people standing on the pier.

Hoarseness invaded his throat. "I . . . I don't know."

I glanced at him and noticed beads of sweat building on his forehead. "Are you okay?"

Myles barely nodded.

I rested my sunglasses on top of my head and squinted. "Is that your mom?"

Before he could answer, applause and cheers erupted. I took a step back, thinking this was a mental health intervention. I had been good though.

Myles latched on to my wrist. "Stay calm. It's nothing bad."

"What are Uncle Bobby and Clara doing here? They don't even know your mom."

Myles made a rolling gesture with his fingers. Then his sister unrolled a banner that read, WILL YOU MARRY ME?

"Eva." Myles dropped to one knee. "I have loved you for a long time. I didn't hang out at your house just for Michael. It was to get close to you as well."

The rhythm of my heartbeat changed, and the tone of the proposal changed. I had forgotten all about Michael and the plan until Myles said his name. He hadn't come around since sometime after I had first visited Dr. Monroe. Maybe he was mad because I had allowed my desire for happiness to distract me from fulfilling the plan. How selfish of me.

The remainder of Myles's words were a blur to me. They must have been something special because when I regained focus, I could hear oohs and aahs.

"Eva, will you do what that sign says?"

It took me a while to respond. I wasn't sure what Michael wanted me to do. I could always call it off. After a long pause, I uttered, "Of course I'll marry you."

Entry 17

Dear Diary:

Wedding planning started out a little rocky. Asking for help was an option, but I wanted to plan by myself every intricate detail of a day that I never thought would be possible.

I spent countless hours surfing the internet and studying every bridal magazine that I could get my hands on. My wedding binder was filled to capacity, disorganized, and nearly impossible to close, much like my mind. Chaos overwhelmed me, but I was determined to conquer the mess.

Tabs and dividers had become my best friends. The tab labeled GUEST LIST caused me to reflect a bit. For me to not have many people in my life, I sure had a lot of friends and family who wanted to be spectators. The sudden attempts at a reunion from the same folks who had ostracized me many years ago were shocking.

As word of my engagement spread, so did my phone number. Darn Uncle Bobby and Clara. Still chatty. My call log registered twenty-two incoming calls. Everyone I spoke with mentioned how proud

Uncle Bobby was of me and how well off I was. I thought maybe they had grown over the years or even started on medication like I had, but then something dawned on me. Each conversation was filled with similarities—a bunch of dry begging. I was certain paranoia had no control over that thought.

"Eva, I'm behind on my taxes. They're about to take my house. I wish I had it like you," Uncle Buster mentioned when he called to make sure I had his address to send his invitation.

Aunt Nora called shortly after him. "Sorry I haven't been around much. My car is in need of repairs."

I had rarely seen or heard from either of them since Uncle Bobby stopped them from attending dinners at their house over their disrespect toward me. Even at other family functions, they still turned their noses up at me.

Aunt Nora ended her call with, "Since you are blessed, don't forget to bless those of us in need." This coming from the same lady who wanted nothing to do with me.

"Okay," exited my mouth before I ended the call.

The nerve of everyone, thinking it was acceptable to ask me for something considering how they practically disowned me. I didn't owe them anything, not even an invitation. Allowing my family to witness my nuptials was a stretch. However, I wanted them to see how I persevered despite their treatment of me.

It wasn't that I was well off. Myles was, but he provided a good life for me and made me feel that what was his was also mine. He worked endless hours securing sports deals and endorsement deals and negotiating contracts. I was proud of what he had accomplished and grateful to reap the benefits. All my estranged family saw were the dollar signs from working alongside prominent athletes. They failed to realize the cons associated with the job. While he made an excellent salary, he was away from home a lot and didn't get to enjoy his success as much as he would have liked.

From a financial standpoint, life with Myles was much different from what I was used to growing up. My mother became a single parent when my father died of a heart attack while at work. I was only two at the time and didn't have any memories of him. We weren't rich, so there wasn't a massive life insurance payout. My once-stay-at-home mother had to take multiple jobs to provide for Michael and me. She worked full-time as the church secretary, and to make extra money, she cleaned high-scale office buildings, similar to the one Myles worked in, on a part-time basis. When payday came every two weeks, she could barely afford to cover bills along with the necessities for my brother and me.

I had never envisioned an upscale life until I found a receipt in Myles's sock drawer while putting away his laundry. My engagement ring cost nearly $40,000. He had already set a $200,000 wedding budget, but the price of the ring took my breath away. It made me feel as if this was standard for wealthy women and I was late for the party.

I didn't know how to enjoy the finer things in life that came with having money. Was I supposed to act like the women I watched on TV? Was I supposed to shop all day, buying nothing but designer clothes, fancy handbags, and red-bottom shoes? Was I supposed to meet up with other women I didn't like just to subtly brag or compare what I had versus what they had? Was I supposed to dine at renowned restaurants, drinking expensive bottles of wine? When we greeted one another, was I supposed to fake kiss them on each cheek? I wondered if there was a manual for newly rich women that I should have read to prepare me.

I didn't care much about the amount of money Myles had. I didn't even know what to do with that much money. I was just excited being a normal girl, planning a fairy-tale wedding that most people only dreamed of.

Questions were asked and rumors swirled about why we were marrying so fast. I was not pregnant, as many speculated. Never lost my virginity. There was only one Mary and one Jesus I knew of. The deadline was swift because I wanted to hurry up and experience a ceremony while I had a chance.

So far, my mental health had been solid, but I never knew when that would change and if Myles would change his mind about me and everything required to be with me.

"Hey, you," Myles interrupted my purge of my wedding planning book. One of his Nikes crossed inches from my face. "Making a mess I see," he said and plopped down on the couch.

"If planning this wedding is making a mess to you, then I guess that's what I'm doing," I snapped.

"It was a joke, Eva."

"I don't have time for jokes, Myles." I pointed at the pictures I had lined up across the edge of the other couch and added, "I still have to finalize the venue, make the cake-tasting appointment, and decide on flowers."

"Can I help with something?"

An irritated huff moved the loose papers strewn across the floor. "I got it."

"Don't go turning into a bridezilla on me. Relax and enjoy the process, babe. I know you women feel the need to do it all, but know that I am here to help. We are a team."

Most women probably would have melted over those words. "Thanks," I dryly replied.

"Speaking of appointments, Dr. Monroe's office called and said you missed yours."

"I know. I've been meaning to reschedule, but it keeps slipping my mind."

"Eva—"

"Please don't start, Myles. I will call first thing in the morning. It's one shot. I will be fine."

He left it alone and moved on to another topic I didn't care to discuss. "Mama said she's called you and left messages, but you won't return her calls. Everything okay there?"

I blew out an exasperated breath once more. The mere sound of Myles's voice worked every nerve in my body. He saw all the papers spread out, which meant I was busy. I never bothered him when he was deep into his work. "Everything is fine. That slipped my mind too." I stretched the truth a bit. I already knew what she had called for, and I was not interested.

"She'd like us to come over. She cooked."

I made sure to hide my eye roll and tried to hide the increased irritation in my voice. "Can you go without me? I really need to get this done."

"Bring it with you. She'd love to help."

Help wasn't what Mrs. Sanders wanted to offer. She had that takeover spirit. The moment Myles proposed, his mother became obsessed with me wearing the dress she got married in. She had hoped to pass it down to Myles's sister, Sheila, but since she was a lesbian who played the masculine role, she insisted I wear it. It may have very well been a lovely dress, but I didn't want to wear it.

"Myles, please. No. Today isn't good."

"I already told her we were coming."

All the dodging I'd done, and Mrs. Sanders had finally cornered me.

Entry 18

Dear Diary:

There was no small talk from Mrs. Sanders when we arrived. She immediately whisked me away to her bedroom. "Here it is," she said as a broad smile revealed her veneers, compliments of Myles.

The dress lay across the bed in a see-through garment bag. From what I could see through the plastic, it was already a definite no from me.

As Mrs. Sanders unzipped the bag, her smile widened more. She was proud, and I didn't want to take that moment away from her. What if my mother were still alive to witness this occasion or to pass her dress down to me? She would have probably worn the same coat of happiness as Mrs. Sanders.

"Wow," I said and covered my mouth, faking my enthusiasm. If I could stick one finger down my throat and release the disgust that churned inside my stomach when I saw it, I would have. Myles would almost certainly call the wedding off.

I hated the dress. It was hideous. In fact, hideous wasn't a strong enough word to describe the dress. It was an old-fashioned, unappealing frock that wasn't worthy of touching my skin. Since Mr. and Mrs. Sanders had only been married for eight months before Myles came along, I was sure she should have chosen another color besides white.

I appeased her and tried the dress on. I had some time to come up with a pleasant excuse as to why I couldn't wear it.

Mrs. Sanders's eyes became misty upon seeing me emerge from the master bathroom wearing the monstrosity. The gown swallowed me. She was no slim lady, and judging by the way the dress fit me, she wasn't back then either.

"Oh, my." She snatched the words right from my mouth, only she added a clap. "You're going to look fabulous."

I wondered if we were looking at the same dress.

"Thank you," I said, tugging at the lace neckline.

Mrs. Sanders stepped into my personal space and started pinning areas that needed adjustments. Practically the entire garment. The lace sleeves traveled well past my fingertips. And the belt loops were supposed to rest across my waistline, but they dangled near my thighs. The tulle on the bottom was ripped in more than one area. So many alterations were needed, yet when I looked into Mrs. Sanders's eyes, it was apparent that we were not on the same page. She still had hope. Her clasped hands rested under her chin. She beamed. I didn't return the sentiment. The dress was not for me. I stared at the floor, scratching and pulling at all the itchy parts.

"You are going to look absolutely beautiful," she said, repeating her approval.

"Thank you so much for this." *Maybe I can pay the alteration shop extra to say they ruined it beyond repair.*

"A good friend of mine is a seamstress, and she has already agreed to complete the alterations free of charge as a wedding gift." Mrs. Sanders cheered, clapped, and lightly bounced on the tips of her toes.

She didn't notice the sarcasm when I said, "I am so lucky."

"I'm going to leave you to change." Mrs. Sanders grabbed my shoulders and pecked my cheek. "I am so happy to take in another daughter."

I felt bad. I didn't know if Mrs. Sanders was aware of my issues, and if she was, she didn't allow it to deter her from welcoming me into the family. Maybe I could take pieces of her dress to make a veil or train. I guess I didn't feel bad enough, because that dress was off me before the door shut good.

Stress overwhelmed me. My hair had started shedding in clumps, my head constantly pounded, and my appetite played hide-and-seek. I plopped on the edge of Mrs. Sanders's bed, contemplating calling off the wedding, possibly postponing it. Things weren't going the way I wanted them to go. Maybe it wasn't meant to be.

"Follow through."

I jumped from the bed, excited. "Michael. You're back."

He didn't respond.

"Michael," I called out, spinning in circles, hoping he'd appear.

"Follow through," he whispered again.

"Will you participate in the wedding? If not, will you at least come?"

I swung around with an attitude when the bedroom door opened without warning.

"Do you need something, honey?" Mrs. Sanders asked.

I gave a half-smile. "No. I'm just finishing up. Thank you."

"I heard you talking, and I thought maybe you needed me."

"Nope. All good," I reassured her, thinking she'd dismiss herself.

Her thin eyebrows met in the middle of her forehead. "Are you sure you're all right?"

I had already told this woman. She was trying to make my life miserable, and I hadn't walked down the aisle yet. Perhaps Myles told her about Michael. I could have lied and said I was on the phone, but it was in my purse, which I left on the foyer table.

"I was just expressing my gratitude for this moment. I didn't realize I was so loud. Thank you again, Mrs. Sanders." I paused and added, "For everything."

She bought it. Her brows returned to their normal position as she modeled her veneers again. Since I suspected she remained by the door to listen, I didn't bother to summon Michael anymore. I returned to the family room with everyone else and pretended like Mrs. Sanders's old wedding dress was the most magnificent piece of fabric I'd ever seen.

Discussing my *Say Yes to the Dress* experience wasn't something I necessarily wanted to do, but Mrs. Sanders had to carry on about it over dinner. "Myles, Eva is going to look stunning in my old gown."

All eyes landed on me and stayed on me until I finished chewing, swallowing, and dabbing the corners of my mouth. "Thank you." I faked a smile.

Mr. Sanders leaned back in his chair and patted his muffin top. "I bet. You were beautiful on that day, baby."

"Aw, that is so sweet," Sheila's girlfriend expressed. Her cheeks swallowed her eyes and turned bright red over her gushing for someone else's love.

I wondered if she had seen the dress and why Mrs. Sanders couldn't have saved it for her. Maybe she had seen it and was excited it went to me instead of her.

Sheila leaned into her elbows and asked, "What do you think of the dress, Eva?"

Did she know? If so, that was uncouth of her to put me on the spot. "It's nice," I lied. "It needs several alterations, so I hope the original look isn't compromised." That sounded believable enough.

Mr. Sanders let out a repulsive belch that spoiled my appetite, wiped the smile from Sheila's girlfriend's face, and rocked the china in the cabinet. Without excusing himself, he added, "Yeah, my wife has always been a brick house. 'She's mighty-mighty.'" He was the only one to chuckle.

And to think I wanted to marry into this family.

Mrs. Sanders tapped the side of her wineglass with a fork. "We have an announcement." She stood. Noncontagious happiness seeped through her entire body. "Well, more like a surprise for the soon-to-be husband and wife."

Not again.

"Since I haven't been needed much for wedding planning, I thought, well, why not surprise the lovebirds with an engagement celebration?"

Sheila and her girlfriend were more excited than I was. I knew Mrs. Sanders meant well, but this was something she should have run by me.

"We helped," Sheila said, pointing between herself and her lady friend.

Was that supposed to make me feel better?

I tried everything in my power to hide my disappointment. At least to where it didn't show on my face. That would've been too obvious. My leg bounced underneath the table. Myles noticed and placed his hand on my knee.

"Thank you guys so much. You all did not have to do this."

"We know. We wanted to do *something*," Mrs. Sanders shadily emphasized.

"Well, Eva and I appreciate it."

Myles needed to speak for himself. He hit my leg under the table, encouraging me to speak up. I cleared my throat. "Yes. We appreciate it." All the lying I did in one night was breaking records.

Myles rubbed his hands together. "Well, let us see."

"Not yet," Sheila yelled. "It's a surprise. Just be dressed and ready when we tell you to. A car will pick y'all up and deliver y'all to the party."

Myles laughed. "Oh, y'all fancy, huh?"

So not only did they go behind our backs and plan a party without any feedback from us, but they wouldn't let us in on the details. I was beyond pissed. "Excuse me, please. I have to use the restroom."

As soon as I rounded the corner, I heard Sheila ask, "Is she upset about the party?"

It was good to see that I wasn't the only liar under this roof. "Nah. She's been under the weather
lately," Myles replied.

Is that what mental health issues mixed with
irritation was called? Under the weather?

"She's not pregnant, is she?" Mrs. Sanders asked

I groaned and made my way to the bathroom.
The cold water that I splashed on my face once
inside did nothing to cool me off. I wanted to slap
everybody at that table. I couldn't believe Myles
was enthused. I couldn't believe Mrs. Sanders
thought I was pregnant. I was not her. I would actually go into my day as a virgin, proudly wearing a
white dress. Just not her white dress.

When I returned to the table, I lied once more. It
had started to become easy. "I don't feel so well. I
think I need to lie down."

"There's fresh linen on the bed in the guest
room," Mrs. Sanders offered.

I should've known Mrs. Sanders would find a
way to keep us here. "Thank you, but I think I'd
like to head on home if that's okay?"

"Very well, hon. I hope you get to feeling better
soon."

"Thank you. And thank you again for a lovely
dinner and for the engagement celebration."

I purposely walked out of the house, leaving
behind that atrocity. We were almost home free

when Mrs. Sanders ran in front of Myles's car like an action hero.

One of her hands flailed in the air. "Wait! You forgot the dress."

I swallowed every ounce of hope. "Oh, wow. I'm so sorry. Thank you so much, Mrs. Sanders."

Entry 19

Dear Diary:

Over the next few productive yet disastrous days, I took Michael's advice. My focus returned to making sure the wedding happened. Everything took a back seat to it, including my rescheduled appointment with Dr. Monroe. Despite the automated message from the office reminding me of the appointment for the following day, it slipped my mind. It was one injection. No harm in missing just one. Plus, I always felt sluggish for a couple of hours after receiving the shot. I didn't have time to slow down. I had a burst of energy that I needed to maintain. I was unstoppable, even without a wink of sleep.

I had prepared three hundred black and gold invites and finalized the seating chart and menus, and all I wanted to do was kick back and people watch for a little while, but Myles once again interrupted.

He plopped down on the chaise beside me, grabbed one of the many wedding books, and started flipping through the tabs. "You should consider becoming a wedding planner," he said with approval covering his face.

I didn't want to talk about the wedding. I needed a mental break. But I mustered up, "Thanks."

I'd kept him out of the loop as much as possible. He paid for everything, so it was up to me to ensure our day would be magical. He knew when and where to show up, and he was fine with it as long as I was happy.

Myles was proud. He was all laughter, jokes, and approval until he scanned over the official guest list. "I see you have Michael's name penciled in. Are you going to place a picture and candle in a chair for him and your mom?"

Crinkles swelled my forehead. "I will for my mother. Why would I do that for Michael?"

Myles's brows crouched. "Hmm," he expressed and moved on. "I'm glad Mr. Bobby is walking you down the aisle. That man loves you like a daughter."

"And hopefully, if Michael comes, they both can. Or Michael can be your best man instead of your dad. Or you can have two."

"You're joking, right?" Myles questioned.

"Um, no. Why would that be a joke?"

"Eva, please don't start this again. You have done so well."

"You're getting on my nerves. What are you talking about?"

"Michael."

"What about him? What's the problem? You don't see me questioning anyone you added to the list." I grew increasingly irritated by the second.

"The people I invited are real people. They are living, breathing, real."

"And Michael isn't?"

Myles blew out a long, deep breath before proceeding with caution. "Eva, no, he isn't. We've been over this several times."

Although he said it as gently as possible, his statement evoked anger. "Say it one more time, Myles. I dare you." I pounded my fist into the palm of my hand, determined to do the same to his face if he didn't control his words.

Michael whispered the most interesting thing. *"Slow and steady wins the race. Slow down, little sister, and keep the pace."*

I laughed. "So you talk in riddles now?"

Myles threw his arms out, confused. "*If* you are talking to *me*, everything I said was perfectly clear. I know you love your brother, but he is no longer with us, Eva. I need you to understand that."

I had forgotten to think and nod when talking to Michael. Sometimes it was just easier to communicate with him as I would with anyone else, and Myles always pissed me off whenever he interrupted our brother-and-sister time.

My head slowly turned to the side. I eyed the armless accent chair. It looked to be too heavy to launch at him. The tall glass vase near the TV, maybe? I remembered trying to move it to clean once. Too heavy. Finally, my eyes settled on the remote. I grabbed it, prepared to impersonate a major league baseball player.

"Listen to me." Michael's voice seemed to come from behind me.

"I'm listening," I replied, still in the pitching position and still forgetting to nod or think.

"What are you listening for? For me to give you an apology? I am not apologizing for making sure you're okay," Myles said.

I didn't bother to tell that nonbeliever that I wasn't talking to him.

"Slow . . . suffer . . . property . . . to him . . . you want." Michael's voice cut in and out like bad cell phone reception.

"Wait! Let me get my book." I ran to the window and retrieved my journal from behind a pillow. "Tell me again," I frantically said. "Tell me again." This time I practically begged.

Myles pulled out his phone, and when I tried to snatch it, my nails scratched his skin, producing specks of blood. The sight of the blood made me want to finish him off. I lunged toward him, but Michael stopped me. *"Not yet."* His whisper was full of static but clear enough for me to understand.

I backed off and paced around the loft, pulling at my box braids and my hair from the root. "Are you calling the police on me again?"

Myles didn't answer. He held the phone to his ear.

"How much longer, Michael?"

"Hi. My name is Myles Sanders calling on behalf of Eva Moss. I wanted to check on her last injection and next appointment," he said and paused, waiting for disappointment.

I stared at him, feeling betrayed. He could've asked me, and I would have told him I missed the routine injection and the rescheduled visit.

"Thank you." Myles disconnected the call. "Eva, get your shoes on."

"For what? I have too much to do for the wedding."

"Dr. Monroe's office is going to squeeze you in."

"What did I just tell you, Myles? I have too much to do."

"Don't go."

"There won't be a wedding if you don't put your shoes on and come on."

That threat scared me.

"Run."

So I did. I ran. And I ran some more. First, I felt throbbing coming from the bottom of my feet. Then, I noticed blood. I sat down in the middle of a busy two-lane road during rush-hour traffic to

see why. By the time I had realized I'd run away
from home without any shoes on, an SUV was
inches away from turning me into roadkill. The
quick-thinking driver swerved and hit a light pole
instead.

"Run," Michael screamed.

I tried, but the pain made it impossible, so
I started crawling. Pain entered my palms and
knees as it did with my feet.

"Ma'am, are you okay?" an older gentleman
asked.

"Run," Michael said and hysterically laughed.

I tried getting up again but fell back down. "I
can't."

"Call a medic. I think she's been hit. She's bleeding," the same gentleman said.

More people hovered around, asking a ton of
questions. I curled up in a fetal position and covered my ears, terrified. I don't remember anything
else from then. I woke up in the psych ward with
bandages covering my hands and feet.

Another hospitalization.

Another release. This time, Uncle Bobby and
Clara were there to pick me up.

My heart dropped, and my knees buckled for
many reasons. "Is Myles okay?"

"Of course, dear." Clara warmly smiled as she
did in just about every situation.

Sadness was in Uncle Bobby's eyes. I think he was disappointed in me.

"Well, if he's okay, then why are you two picking me up? He finally had enough, huh?" I sighed and sobbed into my shirt. "I failed." At that time, I wasn't sure if I had failed at being normal or failed Michael with my lackluster performance.

Clara and her calming voice replied, "Don't worry, sweetheart. Everything is fine. Myles asked us to pick you up while he took care of something."

"Is that something packing up all my things and dropping them off at your house again?" I asked once I was able to stop crying.

"Stop that. Nothing is wrong," Uncle Bobby stepped in to reassure me. It wasn't that I didn't believe Clara, but she always made the worst situations seem like the best situations.

Relieved, I asked, "So he still wants to marry me?"

"Oh, gosh. Of course he does. He's a good man like your Uncle Bobby here," Clara lovingly said and tapped my uncle on his forearm. "Myles would be a fool to leave a lovely young woman who is going to make such a beautiful bride."

I swiped away tears with the sleeve of my shirt. It was refreshing to see that Clara still had a way of making my heart thump at a regular rhythm from the sound of her voice alone. "Do you really mean that?" I asked.

Clara nodded and squeezed me. I wondered if she would still feel the same way once she saw me in my wedding dress. Without question, the dress wouldn't be what anyone expected, especially my soon-to-be mother-in-law.

Mrs. Sanders had reached out to me a couple of times, trying to figure out why I hadn't taken the dress to her friend for alterations.

"I used my mother's sister to feel like my mother was involved," I lied. My mother didn't have a sister.

I had stumbled upon the lifesaving boutique after it was featured on the news as one of the top spots to visit for one-of-a-kind garments. My dress certainly fit that. Initially, I just wanted the owner and seamstress, Zena, to make the necessary changes to what I was expected to wear. I didn't know if it was the bleak look on my face, or my hesitancy to put the dress on as she requested, that caused her to offer some sound advice.

Through a heavy Puerto Rican accent, she said, "Every bride's gown should express their own style and personality, not someone else's. No matter how much I alter this, it will never represent you if this is not what you want." She walked away, leaving me to reflect on her statement.

"How did you know I wasn't happy?" I asked.

"I didn't get featured in the most popular bridal magazine for nothing, honey." She winked.

I instantly fell in love with Zena and her sassiness. From that point on, she and I worked together to sketch the perfect representation of me, and I couldn't wait to show it off.

Entry 20

Dear Diary:

Honoring Michael's wishes became my top priority despite wanting to call off the wedding with each passing day. The constant feelings of revenge conquered my lack of willpower to make it down the aisle. Ever since Myles forced me to get that injection, the warm and fuzzy feelings for him had faded. I wondered if he'd marry me and adopt a controlling spirit and an "I'm the king of this castle" mentality. Sometimes just the sight of him made me sick to my stomach. I played my part, though. Most days were unbearable, but I remembered when I would people watch. I started to channel the many different characters. Soon I became a lead actress in a movie written and directed by my brother. In Myles's face, I was the love of his life who he couldn't wait to marry. Behind his back, I was the one who he'd regret hurting.

"Follow through." I reminded myself of Michael's words while reluctantly preparing for the pre-wedding celebration. I didn't necessarily consider it an engagement party because it was so close to the wedding.

Mrs. Sanders had the nerve to have a swanky invitation requesting our presence at the Ritz-Carlton delivered to us by a local well-known R&B singer, who sang a rendition of Anita Baker's "Sweet Love." An invitation to our own celebration. That was one of the reasons I didn't want her help. Too much. If she wasn't in the mix, she felt a need to try to upstage me. The more Myles gloated over what his mom and sister had done, the more I wanted to puke.

"Babe, Sheila just sent a text. The car will be arriving in five."

It took us a lot longer than five minutes to make it downstairs. Well, mainly me. A part of me hoped that everyone would have grown tired of waiting and left by the time we made it to the party.

"How much longer?" Myles asked again. "Sheila keeps texting me because we haven't made it yet."

"You can go on without me," I said.

Myles looked at me like I was stupid. "That doesn't make any sense. Can you hurry up, please?"

I growled under my breath. I hated being rushed, and I hated being told to hurry up. I didn't ask for this celebration, and my time was just as valuable as theirs.

Almost an hour later, I was finally ready.

The limo driver stood outside the car, waiting patiently. He seemed unbothered by our tardiness. He smiled and opened the door for us. "Good evening, Mr. and soon-to-be Mrs. Sanders."

"'Mrs. Sanders' has a nice ring to it," Myles gushed.

I wasn't so sure I liked being called that. His mother had that name, and I wasn't sure I liked her right now.

Behind my practiced smile was disgust. And I wore that disgust for the entire car ride. If I could have communicated with the limo driver the same way I communicated with Michael, I would have told him to speed up. I couldn't wait to get out of this car. I didn't want to get to the party any faster, either. I just wanted to get away from Myles and the sound of his voice.

"Are you okay?" Myles asked. "You don't seem happy, and you haven't said much."

I started to tell him that I was under the weather, but I didn't bother. "I'm just tired."

I cringed when Myles stroked my hand. "I bet you are tired with all the wedding planning. You have done an excellent job, by the way."

What Myles saw as tiredness was true, but it was from withdrawals. Little did he know, despite getting my injection, which I had no control over, I was no longer taking my oral meds.

Thankfully, we had pulled up in front of the Ritz and I didn't have to listen to any more questions from Myles. Alex Trebek asked fewer of them, and he was a whole game show host. Being pent-up in such a small space with Myles any longer would have made me lose my mind on top of already losing my mind.

I wished the entrance of the hotel was on my side so I could get out faster. But it was on Myles's side. Before the driver opened the door to let us out, Myles leaned over and planted a sloppy kiss on me. Was it sloppy, or was that how I perceived it because I didn't want that attention from him? I wiped the kiss off and noticed Myles hang his head. I just knew an argument was about to start. Nonetheless, he remained a gentleman. He stepped out of the car and reached for my hand to help me out. I hesitated at first. If I grabbed his hand, would I cringe again? Would that, too, be noticeable?

This is only temporary discomfort. Remember the bigger picture. I repeated that in my head a few times before grabbing Myles's hand and exiting the car.

As we walked inside, Myles said, "I don't know if it's the crowd, but I can tell you're uncomfortable. We can speak and leave if that will make you feel better. I just don't want to upset my mother with all the hard work she and my sister put into this."

Of course he didn't want to upset his mother. I had to remind myself that I wasn't Eva but a character in a movie. "Action," I whispered to myself and did what I usually would do—pretend.

The venue was decorated more like an actual wedding reception than an engagement party. I must say, Mrs. Sanders and Sheila went all out for us. Pure elegance. Candles dimly lit the room. White orchids sat on the thick white linen blanketing the round tables. Even the guests had dressed in white. Myles and I were the only oddballs.

"We didn't get the all-white memo," he said to his mom as he leaned in to hug her.

She released her embrace from Myles and grabbed his hand and mine. "It wasn't intended for the two of you to wear white. I wanted y'all to stand out, to be the center of attention, if you will." She glanced at me. "So what do you think?"

"Breathtaking," I said. "Thank you so much."

Mrs. Sanders seemed happy that she got praise from me and everyone else. It was a beautiful setup, but I was ready to go.

I scanned the room, taking in all the details, and that was when I noticed Sabrina Davis. I was sure it was Mrs. Sanders who thought it would be a good idea to invite Myles's ex-fiancé to our engagement party. She stood out not only because she was a few feet away, waiting to approach Myles, but this heifer was the only guest who wore something other than white. Her revealing yellow dress, which barely covered her nipples, had everyone staring, including me. The ruby red form-fitting dress that hugged what little curves I had attached to my size-six frame was nothing compared to her build. She looked like a video vixen with the perfect waist-to-hip ratio. And don't get me started on her hair. Her mane was so silky, and from where I stood, it looked like it was as soft as a bag of feathers.

My hair was naturally curly and pulled up into a messy bun as usual. After seeing how well Sabrina was put together, I wished I would've taken Myles up on his offer of sending me in for a makeover. Instead, I became offended, thinking he thought I wasn't pretty enough.

My eyes shifted to Myles. I needed to see his reaction when he noticed her. Would he stare? Would lust overtake him? Would he want her back? I mean, he was engaged to the woman at one point. The old shoebox that I found stored in his closet held photos of them, and they seemed so happy. He still loved her. He had to. Why else would he have kept the pictures? Maybe he secretly yearned for her to come back to him. They only called off the engagement because Sabrina decided to pursue her passion for missionary work in Africa.

"Hey, bighead," Sabrina said. Their embrace seemed never-ending.

The moment I cleared my throat, I became visible to them.

There was perspiration on Myles's forehead. "I'm sorry," he said. He grabbed my hand and introduced me. "This is my fiancée, Eva."

Sabrina smiled and then hugged me. My hands remained at my sides. I wondered if Myles had been with her when I was in the hospital.

"It's a pleasure to meet you finally," Sabrina said to me. She then looked at Myles, gave him a double nudge, and said, "You did good."

"Yes, she is a dream come true," Myles said.

Did he really mean that? After everything I had put him through? I bet Sabrina never left physical scars. I bet Sabrina didn't have to take medication to fit in.

The gathering was supposed to be about me, and Sabrina managed to outshine me in every aspect. The Sanders family seemed more thrilled to see her than me. I wondered if they hoped that Myles and Sabrina got back together. I wondered if this was the reason she was here. Were they trying to force me out? Persuade him to leave me?

I'd had enough of the reminiscing between Myles, Sabrina, and the other Sanderses. I grabbed his hand and forcefully escorted him to the patio.

"Is everything okay?" he asked.

"Why is she here?" I hissed. "Why did she wear yellow when I'm sure she was told to wear white?"

"What's the big deal?"

"Seriously, Myles. Why would your mom invite her?"

"You would have to ask my mother. I don't see what the harm is."

"I don't want her here. She has to go."

Myles frowned and threw his hands out to his sides. "Come on, babe," he said and reached for my hand. "It would be rude to make her leave. She's not hurting anyone by being here."

"She's hurting me. Do you want to be with her or something?" I asked.

The wrinkles in Myles's forehead deepened. "What? Where is that coming from?"

I inched closer to him, ready to slap the stupid out of him. "Do you want to be with her or not?"

He puckered his lips. "Be for real, Eva."

"You tell the truth, Myles."

Myles massaged his temples. "Eva, please, can we just enjoy the night? Can you just pretend she is not here if her presence bothers you so much?"

"You have a problem pretending. You've carried on a conversation with her longer than you have with me, or anyone else for that matter."

He threw his hands in the air. "What do you want me to do?" he asked as if I hadn't already given him a solution to the problem.

"She needs to go." I folded my arms across my chest and shifted all my weight to one foot.

Myles shook his head in disbelief and walked inside, leaving me alone. I didn't mind being by myself. I needed some advice from my brother anyway.

"Michael, can you hear me?" I waited for a response. Moments passed before I called out to him again. "Michael, if you can hear me, please say something."

Suddenly, footsteps approached from the walkway opposite the patio. My heart fluttered, thinking I'd actually get to see my brother after all these years. He never revealed himself to me because, according to him, the car accident left him disfigured and he didn't want me to see him that way.

"Michael, is that you?" I asked. "We need to change the plan."

The steps got closer.

I tried peering around the bushes that lined the walkway, but it was too dark.

"Michael, is that you?" I whispered.

"No, it's just me, Sabrina."

Luckily, the globe lights strung from one side to the other didn't produce enough light for Sabrina to notice my quivering body. "How long have you been standing there?" I hoped she didn't detect the nervous cracking in my voice.

"Long enough. Who is Michael, and what's the plan?"

Suddenly offended that she had the audacity to question me, I snapped, "None of your business. You need to leave."

She laughed. "I'm not going anywhere. I was invited." Her hands rested on her hips while she tapped her shoe against the cobblestone-covered patio, demanding an answer.

This chick had come into my celebration, hogged the attention, and demanded answers from me. I was not going to allow her to continue to control me or this situation.

"Well, I don't want you here, and I am about to make sure the Sanderses know it, too." I pivoted and started my march inside. Sabrina was hot on my heels. I turned around and blocked the door. "Is there something I can help you with?" I asked.

"In fact, there is," she said. "You can start by telling me your motives. Who is Michael to you, and what's the plan?"

"Why is it any of your business?"

"It's my business because—"

"Because what? Do you want Myles back? Because if you do, it won't happen. He's with me now, so deal with it." I waved my sparkling diamond ring around to make sure she understood that I had him and unless I let him go, she didn't stand a chance.

We stared one another down. Sabrina got bold and took a step toward me, and I took a few toward her. She should've asked Myles what I was capable of.

"Does Myles know about Michael?"

"I don't owe you an explanation. Since you want to know so bad, Michael is my married lover," I lied with motives.

She smirked and stepped back. "We will see how the Sanderses feel about Michael."

She took the bait. Her stilettos clicked the ground at a rapid pace as she marched inside. I peered through the doors of the patio. Sabrina did just what I expected. She walked right up to them in hopes of destroying my relationship with her ex. There was nothing I needed to do. She was about to get rid of herself as soon as she made the crazy accusation that I was having an affair with my brother.

How convenient for Miss Thang. Except for Myles, the Sanderses were all together, posing for a picture. I wished I could read her black-painted lips that moved at a high rate of speed. It would have at least given me a head start on my next move. I crossed my fingers, hoping they'd remove her from the party once they heard her ridiculous version of who she thought Michael was to me. From what I could see, they seemed to take no interest in what she had to say.

Sabrina disappeared for a moment, but then she reemerged in front of me. The only thing that separated us was the glass patio door.

I smiled at her and hurled some insults her way. "How did that work out for you, you stupid home-wrecker slut?" I didn't know whether she heard them. It just felt good to get them out.

She forced her way onto the patio, waving her hands around, upset. Whatever she said was muffled and irrelevant.

"You can say whatever you want to say, Sabrina. The Sanderses will never believe you anyway."

"Sabrina?" Myles said from behind me.

I was so engaged with his ex that I didn't hear Myles approaching.

I turned to Myles. "You hear her disrespecting me? She needs to leave."

Tears poured from Myles's eyes. "I think we've had enough for the night." His voice cracked.

I had to have the last word. "You heard my man. You need to leave." He didn't exactly say those words, but that was what needed to happen. It should have happened a long time ago. She should have never been invited in the first place.

Myles extended his hand and said, "Come on, Eva, we are leaving."

He chose me. I turned back to Sabrina to make sure she understood once and for all, but she was gone.

"Come on, Eva." Myles's voice was soft, and tears still ran from their home.

"Why are we leaving?" I asked, confused. "She was the one trying to ruin our engagement celebration."

"Let's just go," he said, motioning me to take his hand. "We can talk in the car."

"Okay. Let me tell everyone bye."

"We will thank them later. Let's just go."

That was fine by me. I didn't necessarily want to talk to anyone, but it was the polite thing to do.

Myles and I held hands and walked around the building to his sister's two-seater convertible Jag. "We aren't going back in the limo?" I questioned.

"Nah. The limo is going to take Sheila home," Myles answered.

Myles was never this quiet unless something bothered him. I assumed it was the altercation with Sabrina, so I tried making small talk with him so he'd know that I wasn't upset with him. "Did you enjoy the party?" I asked.

He shrugged.

"Look, I'm not mad about Sabrina. But I think you should talk with your mother. She overstepped."

Myles heavily sighed. "When was the last time you took your medicine?"

Typical. He tried to make the situation about me and my illness, which upset me. "What does that have to do with anything? Your primary concern should be the way Sabrina acted toward me."

"Okay, Eva."

"Are you still seeing her?"

No response.

"I know you hear me talking to you, Myles Sanders."

Still, no response.

The fact that he ignored me angered me. I fought back the desire to hit him. I thought back to the techniques I learned from my therapist to calm down once I reached a certain point. Those points were boiling now. I tried breathing. I tried replacing negative thinking with positives. It wasn't working.

I'd finally had enough and needed to lash out physically. Instead of hitting Myles, I started repeatedly smacking myself in the face. "Answer me, Myles. Are you and Sabrina seeing each other?" My throat burned from screaming at him.

He sped up the car and still pretended as if he didn't hear me.

My throat and face shared the same burn. "All night, you spent time getting *reacquainted* with Sabrina instead of celebrating with me. I saw the way you were looking at her in that provocative, inappropriate dress. Lust was in your eyes."

It wasn't until the car came to an abrupt halt that I realized we were at the emergency room. I laughed. "Again, Myles? Is this so you can go be with Sabrina?"

He shook his head. "This is so you can get better."

"I'm not getting out."

Myles turned the car off and took the keys with him. The hospital doors automatically opened, but he didn't go inside. I saw his mouth moving, and a few minutes later, hospital staff approached with a wheelchair. I wasn't having a baby, nor was I paralyzed. I should have run.

"Hi, Ms. Moss," the nurse spoke.

"I'm not getting out."

The same soft-spoken nurse asked, "Will you please come in and let me take your vitals and ask you a few questions?"

"I don't see a need for that. Why does everyone think something is wrong with me? Am I not allowed to be upset because the man I am supposed to marry allowed his ex-fiancée, Sabrina, and her hookerish yellow dress to ruin our engagement party?"

The nurse looked at Myles like she wanted an explanation.

"The only person who wore yellow was my elderly high school social studies teacher. A yellow pantsuit, to be exact. She and I spent some of the night catching up, yes." Somberness overtook his eyes before he added, "And as far as Sabrina, she died from malaria while in Africa years ago."

Entry 21

Dear Diary:

"Hey," I greeted Myles.

"Hey." He rose from the couch to hug me. It wasn't a lingering hug like usual. "Sorry I wasn't able to pick you up from the hospital. I had a meeting at the office."

"It's okay. That was the first thing Clara told me when she picked me up." Surprisingly, it was just Clara who picked me up. Although she said Uncle Bobby had a doctor's appointment, I felt otherwise. Like maybe he had grown tired of this same song and dance with me.

"How are you feeling?" Myles eased out.

I shrugged. "I'm okay, I guess. Tired and embarrassed."

Myles patted the couch. "Sit. Let's talk."

My heart slid to my stomach. I just knew he was about to call off the wedding. That was probably for the best anyway. Myles deserved so much better than what I had to offer.

"Can I take a shower first? I'll make it quick." Something about being in a mental institution made me feel as if I needed to scrub the stench of crazy off me as soon as I got home. The hospital carried a distinct aroma—a combination of bleach and urine. Every time I was discharged, the smell was discharged with me.

Myles nodded. "You don't have to rush."

I took a long shower, followed by a long bath and another shower. Myles was still in the same spot when I emerged from my room saturated in perfume and with one of his T-shirts on that fit me like a gown. "Sorry. I'm ready." He patted the same place on the couch, and I sat. In between us was a wooden box. "What's this?" I nervously asked.

"I'm going to show you," he said and powered off the TV.

I gulped. We'd never had a conversation where the tension could be felt over the usual cozy atmosphere of our den.

He cleared his throat and pushed the wooden box closer to me. "Open it."

I hesitated because I was afraid of what was inside. My hands quivered when I touched the box. Inside was a program folded in half. I gasped and instantly started crying when I unfolded the program and saw Sabrina's name and face. Myles cried too. He had to show me her obituary to make it make sense.

I shook my head, hoping to shake away the humiliation. "I am so sorry, Myles. The hallucinations seemed so real." An entire fake scenario had played out in my mind.

He rubbed my shoulder. "We are going to get through this. You have to be consistent with your medicine. You can't pick and choose. It has to stay in your system for you to be stable and healthy. I am about to be your husband. You can talk to me about these things."

I blushed a little. "Not too many people are this understanding. I just—"

He covered my mouth with his hand to silence me. "I will always be here for you. Don't get yourself so worked up over this. You have a support system."

"And I'm sure my support system is tired of me messing up."

"Don't say that, Eva. Like I said, you just need to make sure you get into a routine so that you don't forget to take your meds. Never think that I won't be here for you. That's what marriage is all about."

"Are you sure getting married is the right thing to do? You are handsome and successful and can have any girl you want, yet you are stressed out over dealing with me."

Myles frowned. "If I didn't want to marry you, then I would have never asked. Yeah, things are sometimes a little rough, but when they aren't, things are great. If we both do our part, I believe we will have more great days than not."

I nodded, still not understanding what Myles saw in me. I was crazy, just like my family always said.

"Speaking of the wedding, your seamstress has blown your phone up looking for you."

I jumped up. "Oh, shoot, what's today's date? Where's my phone?" Dates aren't a thing a person keeps up with when they are not in their right mind.

Myles pointed. "On the dining room table."

"Did you tell her where I was?"

"No. It's not my business to tell. Besides, I thought my mom's friend was making the alterations."

"Yeah, about that. I went in a different direction."

"Does my mom know?"

"We hadn't discussed it."

"So, no?"

"No."

"Can you please tell her so she won't feel as if she was left in the dark?"

"I will," I lied again. I didn't plan on telling Mrs. Sanders anything. Whenever it came up later, I'd chalk it up to memory loss or something along those lines.

I heard bits and pieces of what Myles said, but I was more focused on trying to get Zena on the phone, to no avail. Glancing at the clock on the wall, I only had about forty minutes to make it there. "I have to go. I have to get to the alteration shop."

"I can drive you."

"No!" I didn't mean to scream my objection. "I'm sorry. I don't want you to see it before the wedding."

"I understand. Before you go, I have a surprise for you," Myles said.

I didn't have time for surprises, but I obliged. "What kind of surprise?"

"Can I have a kiss first?" He puckered his lips, and I quickly pecked them.

"Okay, now where's my surprise?" I was antsy like a child. Plus, I had to go.

"Close your eyes," he instructed.

I groaned. "Just show me. Don't drag it out."

"If you want to see it, then close your eyes."

I let out a puff of air and closed them.

A few seconds passed. "Okay, you can open them now."

I gasped, covered my mouth, and backed away. Tears heavily rolled down my face.

"Mi . . . It's Michael." I pointed to Myles's new chest tattoo.

"It is, babe. I got your brother tattooed on me so he'll always be with us."

Words got lost on the way to my mouth. Finally, after the sobs dried up and the words found their way back to me, I asked, "Why would you do that?"

"I wanted to memorialize Michael to show you how important he was to me. He was my brother, and with his face on my chest, we can both see him and feel that connection to him every day."

I shook my head at a loss for words again.

"We are going to be okay," Myles kissed my forehead and assured me. "Well, hurry back," Myles said. "I was hoping we could order some takeout and watch a movie."

I smiled. "I'd love that. Be right back." I grabbed my purse and headed toward the door.

Myles stopped me. "Babe. Pants."

"Shoot." I was in such a hurry to get to Zena that I had forgotten I only had on Myles's shirt. I threw on a pair of sweats, channeled my old track days to get to the car, and cut the usual twenty-minute drive in half.

Fortunately for me, I got out of the hospital in enough time to pick my dress up from Zena's shop. Had Myles not mentioned it, I would've missed the deadline to have the necessary last-minute modifications made if needed.

One thing about Zena, she stayed true to her business hours. The sign read a closing time of five o'clock, but she began making announcements and locking the door around four forty-five.

"We're closed," Zena said upon hearing the door chime when I entered the boutique one minute before she locked up.

She never took her eyes from the computer until I announced myself. "Zena, it's me, Eva."

"Girl, you were supposed to pick this dress up days ago. Where have you been?"

The shrugging would have to suffice. It wasn't any of her business where I had been.

"Don't tell me you have cold feet. I know it's not the dress because I only prepare the best," she said, snapping her fingers twice. "So is it the man?" she asked and went on a wild rant. "Men are trash. I'm not saying there aren't any good ones, but they are hard to find. They always claim they want to find the one but forget one is one, not one and some possibles. That's why I'm single, honey."

"He didn't do anything."

She looked me up and down. "So was it you? Did you cheat on that good man?"

Zena just went on a rant about how there weren't any good men, but . . . never mind. "No, I didn't cheat."

"Uh-huh. So what then? I called your phone a lot."

It seemed as if she would continue prying until I gave her something. "Just been a little under the weather, but I'm better now."

She looked me up and down again. "Yeah, sure, whatever you say."

While she retrieved my dress from the back, I stared at myself in the fitting room mirror. How did I get here? A place that many girls dreamed of was happening to me. I never thought I would find the perfect guy, the perfect dress, the perfect ceremony, and while I was surrounded by so much perfection, my groom wouldn't be receiving perfect reviews in return.

Zena broke through my thoughts. "Here it is." She hung the garment bag on the door and left me to it.

Once I slipped into the dress and allowed Zena to adjust my train, I marveled at how it turned out, and I couldn't wait for Myles to see me in it. Dresses weren't my thing unless they had to be, but I admired how this dress lay on my body. The thought of how my life would be as a wife crossed my mind. Would I cook? Clean? Or would I be like the reality stars, shop, show off my wealth on social media all day, and meet at fancy coffeehouses several times a week?

Zena's voice silenced the fantasies. "What do you think, girlie?"

I spun around, allowing her the opportunity to assess her finished creation. "I think this may get you another magazine mention."

She popped her collar, knowing that she'd done it once again.

"Thank you so much for making my dress, Zena."

"Thank you for trusting the process. You are going to make a beautiful bride. Now hurry up and get your ass out of my shop. You know I lock up early."

"Beautiful bride" was a compliment that I'd heard a lot. Hopefully, that same sentiment applied when they saw me all put together. I folded the oversized garment bag over my forearm and turned to Zena. "See you in two Saturdays, right?" I confirmed.

"Wedding starts at three o'clock, but you want me there at one, right?" Zena confirmed.

"Right."

"I wouldn't miss it for the world."

In the beginning, Zena was just my seamstress, but as the months passed, she'd become so much more than that. More like my first-ever girlfriend and makeup artist.

Entry 22

Dear Diary:

Being that our wedding party only consisted of Uncle Bobby, who was to walk me down the aisle, Clara, who was to serve as my matron of honor, and Mr. Sanders, who stood alongside Myles as the best man, there wasn't much of a rehearsal needed. Plus, I wasn't in the mood to be bothered by people. I had hoped that things would be on the upswing, but after my last hospitalization and follow-up with Dr. Monroe, he increased the milligrams of my antipsychotic. According to the good doc, the missed injection coupled with the missed medication, along with wedding stress, had thrown me off-balance a little. I tried taking it as prescribed, but it had me feeling like a zombie, and I had to listen to my body at least until I got through the wedding and honeymoon.

Myles called himself being supportive, but I think he was trying to be low-key slick and babysit me. "How about we set our phones for the same time each day as a reminder for you to take your meds and me to take my vitamins?"

To avoid an argument, I agreed. We set a daily reminder. Every morning, we'd eat breakfast, and Myles would watch me swallow Tic Tacs. He never suspected a thing. It was only supposed to be temporary, but I liked feeling sluggish from being off-balance more than sluggish from being overly medicated.

As I sat standoffishly in a chair of the wedding venue before the start of the rehearsal, I contemplated if I had enough in me to go through with it. My emotions ran wild. My body felt beaten down, and those whispers were back. Not Michael's voice, though. That brother of mine hadn't resurfaced for a while.

"Good evening. I am Pamela, and I'd like to thank you, Myles and Eva, for trusting me with coordinating a wedding you will always remember."

If it were left up to me, there would be no wedding coordinator. Because I'd fallen ill a few times, Myles thought it would be a good idea to bring someone in to keep things running smoothly. I appreciated his effort, but I didn't care for her. I especially didn't like the way she pranced around like a ballerina, barking orders at us.

"Let's start with prayer if you don't mind." Pamela placed the clipboard she held on the podium, tucked her shoulder-length salt-and-pepper hair behind her ears, and immediately clasped her hands together.

I raised my hand. "Excuse me," I said. Without giving her a chance to acknowledge my interruption, I added, "I mind."

"Oh, no she didn't," Sheila said, referring to my refusal.

"I'd like to move it along," I added and tossed a smug look in Sheila's direction. This was my wedding, not hers, and I would do what I wanted.

"As you wish," Pamela said, clearly disappointed. "Can I have Myles and his handsome father practice marching in from this door?" She brushed her hand across Myles's shoulder as she instructed him. "When you and your father exit, you will stand here." She pointed to a spot at the makeshift altar. Then she grabbed hold of his hand and walked him to the place she had just pointed out.

I didn't understand why she felt a need to keep touching my man.

"Ms. Eva, let's run through your part." Pamela smiled at me like she wasn't just practically throwing herself at Myles, knowing he was with me.

I heard her, but I didn't move. "I already know what to do."

Sheila scoffed. Pamela's eyes bucked as if to say, "I know she ain't talking to me like that." I totally was.

After about thirty minutes of everyone but me rehearsing roles, we headed out to dinner. It was there that Myles leaned over to me and planted a lingering kiss on my cheek. Then he whispered into my ear, "After the wedding, I know things will return to normal."

He was still under the impression that my most recent mishap occurred because of wedding planning. What about all the other times? After witnessing some pretty erratic behavior, he still didn't understand that his version of normal and my version of normal were two different things. Normal for me was exactly what he saw. Normal for me was exactly what I lived. The ups and downs were a part of me, a part of who I was, no matter if I or anyone else was willing to accept that. Sometimes I thought maybe I would have expected more out of life if my expectations were different. I was a product of my surroundings, and whatever my family said I believed to be true.

Since my family knew my secret and decided to crash the rehearsal dinner when I felt low, I was sure everyone who didn't know would find out.

I heard them before I saw them.

"Whew, this is a fancy shindig." The rasp in Uncle Buster's voice hadn't changed.

I snapped at Uncle Bobby and Clara, "What are they doing here? This dinner is supposed to be for the wedding party only."

"I know. I know, but they were at the house earlier and asked if they could come. I didn't think you'd mind," Clara said.

Her sweet tone was not working on me. I had never been disrespectful to Clara before, but I inhaled, prepared to let her have it.

"Babe," Myles said, "it's okay. The more the merrier."

I rolled my eyes and lost my appetite as Myles stood and greeted Uncle Buster, Aunt Nora, and her loud-mouthed friend.

"You must be the rich one. You look rich," Uncle Buster uncouthly remarked and complimented Myles's pink polo shirt.

Myles laughed. "I wouldn't say all that. I do okay for myself."

Not only did Myles do well for himself, but he did well for the both of us. So much so that he allowed me to quit my fake job. I always had money thanks to my monthly social security checks, so he never found out that I had never worked a day in my life.

Uncle Buster had the audacity to pat Myles's pocket and say, "Let me get a couple dollars off of you." He laughed hysterically, and so did Myles and a few others. Little did they know, Uncle Buster was serious. Had Myles opened his wallet, Uncle Buster would have accepted.

"Yummy." Aunt Nora's friend pushed up her saggy breasts and sensually licked her lips. "You are a good-looking fella. Got any uncles my age who look like you?"

Myles laughed again. "I appreciate that, ma'am." He leaned in and pecked the back of her hand.

"Don't age me. Call me Lynn. And call me if—"

Uncle Buster interrupted. "Girl, get your old ass on somewhere."

"Nora. Eva's aunt. I helped to raise her. Remember that." She held her hand out, awaiting the same gesture that Myles had given her friend.

That sucker did it. He pecked Aunt Nora's hand twice. "It's a pleasure to meet you as well. And thank you for taking care of my fiancée."

"I helped," Aunt Nora's friend said, adding in a lie of her own.

"Thank you all," Myles said and sat down.

With the mood I was in, they weren't going to get away with lying. First, I started with Aunt Nora's friend. "You said you helped to raise me?"

She nervously giggled and fanned me off. "Oh. You know it takes a village."

"Exactly what did you do? If I remember correctly, you didn't want me unless I came with state benefits or an inheritance. Truth be told, I never knew what your name was until tonight, and as far as I'm concerned, you don't have enough of my respect for me to consider you as anything more than Aunt Nora's friend."

Everyone stared at me in disbelief. I was just getting started.

"Babe," Myles said and placed his hand on my knee to calm me down. I never knew why he always did that. I was going to do and say whatever I wanted, and no hand to the knee would stop that.

"No. I waited years to get this off of my chest, and since they are here, they might as well hear it."

"Oh, dear. How about a bathroom break?" Clara tried, but I wasn't trying to hear her either.

"And, Aunt Nora, how dare you tell that lie? If you helped to raise me, then tell me why I never saw you after Uncle Bobby banned you from his house because you couldn't stop saying upsetting things about me."

She peered at me over the free glass of red wine she sipped.

Uncle Buster was next. He held his hands up to silence me, but I couldn't be stopped. "And you. You are nothing more than a poor excuse of a man," I told him. "Uncle Bobby was a great father figure and protector. You should try to be more like him."

"Eva, enough," Myles demanded. "Not here."

"Why?" I asked. "They can sit around and call me out, but when I do it, I'm silenced."

Myles's entire family had the stank face. So did the three amigos.

"Come on, let's get some fresh air," Myles suggested.

"The air is fine in here." There was no reason for me to leave my own rehearsal dinner. My fake family should have been the ones to leave.

"We have a bridezilla on our hands." What was meant to be a whisper by Aunt Nora turned out to be her regular voice. Nothing had changed. She still hadn't learned the art of a whisper.

"I think it's best we call it a night. We all have a busy day tomorrow, and we should probably get some rest," Uncle Bobby insisted. That was his way of separating me from the phony people. I appreciated him once again for stepping up to be my protector—something Myles should have done. But he was too busy kissing hands and asses to realize he should have been on my side.

"Good idea, Uncle Bobby."

"Does this mean we can't come to the wedding? We were invited," Uncle Buster asked Myles on his way out.

They were always so afraid of me, so I wondered why they were so pressed to attend my wedding.

He stood and shook Uncle Buster's hand. "I'll see you tomorrow, man."

I shook my head, disgusted. Good thing I didn't have to see Myles anymore for the rest of the evening. He was staying at the Ritz, where the ceremony was to be held, and I was staying at the loft with Clara.

The rest of the dinner was quiet. I didn't eat any of the steak or baked potato that was served to us like everyone else did. A couple of people even asked for seconds, while Myles ate off my plate. I sipped multiple glasses of wine, though.

"Babe, slow down on the wine," Myles whispered into my ear. "It will interfere with your medication."

I stared at him as I poured more into my glass. There was no medication to interfere with. But I had to play the part. "Last glass, I promise."

All I remembered was staggering to Clara's car before jolting from my sleep.

"Finish him."

I jumped up, sweating over the loud command.

"Michael," I whispered, careful not to alarm Clara.

"Finish him," he said again.

I kept my volume at a whisper. "Michael, where have you been?"

"Finish him."

"How? How am I supposed to do it? Do I call the wedding off or what?"

Michael had a way of popping in and popping out without much explanation. He held the blueprint, but he never made it clear. I must have called his name a million times, but he was gone. I stayed up all night, pacing my bedroom floor, thinking.

I wondered how life would have turned out had Michael and Myles remained best friends. It was evident that Myles loved me, no matter my shortcomings. I loved him, no matter how much of a punk he was. I was sure we would have been together, and with Michael's approval. Unfortunately, Myles had to go. No backing down. No negotiating.

Entry 23

Dear Diary:

Myles had been nothing but good to me. I wished I didn't have to hurt him. I wished he could have found the love he deserved. I knew I was not the one for him. I never understood what his infatuation was with me, anyway. The moment we reconnected, his obsession with me picked up where it left off.

The slight shaking of my shoulder shifted my focus back into the room. "Where did you zone out to?" Zena asked.

"I'm sorry. My mind is elsewhere," I said through a slight giggle.

"I see. What do you think?" She passed me a hand mirror.

I gasped. "Zena, I love it. It's so elegant." She'd taken my long hair that hung down the middle of my back and transformed it into a two-strand braid with a few dangling curls.

I looked around and noticed that, while I was daydreaming, the room had filled with unauthorized people. I blinked to make sure I wasn't seeing things. I wasn't. Mrs. Sanders and her crew of old lady friends were there. They were headed my way.

"Here we go," I mumbled, but I smiled and played the part of an excited bride once they surrounded me.

"We were hoping to have a moment of prayer with you," Mrs. Sanders said.

A tiny voice added, "And be privileged enough to steal a glimpse of you all dolled up before everyone else. I really cannot wait to see how wonderful my best friend's dress is going to look on you."

Another comment about that stupid dress. I thought maybe it was just me and my taste when it came to fashion. But I remembered Zena didn't like the dress either, and she was a style icon. Instead of wedding gifts, we asked that everyone donate to whatever charity Myles and I chose, but we should have encouraged everyone to get eye exams. That wedding dress was not cute. Not even just a little bit. And I wanted to understand what they saw.

Making an assumption because of my hesitancy to accept their request for prayer, one of the old ladies asked, "You believe, don't you?"

Mrs. Sanders interjected, "Of course she does. My son knows I wouldn't have it any other way."

She didn't know me at all, but I let her have the moment. Soon the pressure would be on her

Because in less than an hour, she'd have to face questions as to why I wasn't wearing her dress. Neither prayer nor the Lord were my thing. If He existed, then why would He make me this way? Why would He take my family away? Why would He allow people to judge me if I was ill? Why wouldn't He place more people in my life who understood me and what I struggled with? And most importantly, why would He allow someone to create the ensemble worn by my future mother-in-law?

While they had their eyes closed and heads bowed, thanking the Lord for all that He had done and would do, I stared at them, wondering how much of what they said they actually believed. I wondered what personal problems they had in life that weren't being fixed by the invisible Savior they begged to. The prayer went on for what seemed like forever, and I went along with it. I giggled on the inside when they cried out and spoke in tongues. People really talked like that outside of the fake religious infomercials.

All of a sudden, wetness hit me. "What the hell?" I said as I wiped away the moisture from my forehead.

Mrs. Sanders and her friends let out a chorus of gasps. They were shocked. Some of them drew a cross symbol on their foreheads. One clutched her cross necklace. And one apologized to God and asked for forgiveness on my behalf because of the language that I had used around His children.

Attempting to restore the peace, Mrs. Sanders said, "Now, now, everyone settle down." She faced me and calmly requested that I apologize to the room for what I had just blurted out. "Eva," she delicately called, "I know that you have been under an extreme amount of stress, but I and my group of friends do not use language like that, nor do we like to hear it. I'm sure with your mother being a Christian and all, she taught you to respect your elders. An apology is very necessary."

Feeling insulted because not only did she speak to me condescendingly, but she brought my mother into it, I just stared at her. I wanted to slap her in the same manner I did her son.

I twisted in my seat when one of Mrs. Sanders's old homegirls asked, "Do you hear your mother talking to you, child?"

I inhaled. My chest rose high, like breath had been blown into a CPR doll. "First of all—"

"Look at the time," Zena said, holding on to my shoulder with one hand so that I remained in my seat. She glanced at her wrist, which had no watch.

That lady got blessed and didn't realize it. None of them realized it, because they all still stood in my face, assumingly waiting for an apology that wasn't coming.

"We must get this bride into her gown. Will everyone please take their seats inside the sanctuary?" They were slow to move, but Zena meant business. She didn't let up with her shrewd comments and barking of orders until everyone was gone—everyone except Mrs. Sanders.

"Can you get rid of her too, Zena?" I demanded as if she were my servant.

"Mother of the groom," she said, approaching Mrs. Sanders delicately, "your presence is needed inside."

Her eyes lightly rolled. "And you are, dear?"

"I'm sorry. I'm Zena, the seamstress, designer, and hair stylist. I do it all. I am also going to help Eva into her dress and apply her makeup."

"Oh. You are the aunt who made alterations to *my* dress."

Zena peeked over her shoulder at me. It was kind of like she was asking permission to answer the question.

I shrugged. That was my way of saying I didn't care what she said because she would find out soon anyway.

"Something like that," Zena said. "Now, if I could get you to take your seat, I can get this beautiful lady dressed."

Mrs. Sanders remained seated. "I was hoping to get a glimpse ahead of everyone else. I'm sure Eva won't mind." She looked at me with hope in her eyes.

Her persistence didn't pay off. Zena had a come-back for that, too. "I understand, but she wanted to surprise you once she was all put together. Right, Eva?"

I nodded.

"Very well," she said. She gathered her things and left.

Finally, it was just Zena and me, and I had a lot to say. "I don't know who that old lady thought she was talking to. I am not a child, and Mrs. Sanders was nowhere near my mother and will never be. Mother-in-law, yes. But . . ." I stopped before add-ing how that was only a temporary arrangement. Myles would make me a widow in no time, so the title didn't really count.

"Don't let these people get under your skin," Zena said. "This is your day. They will be okay."

"I cannot thank you enough," I told her. "Who in their right mind thinks it's okay to throw cooking oil on a person's face?" I glanced in the mirror and noticed a red mark on my forehead from attempt-ing to scrub my skin off.

Zena buckled over with laughter. "It's just anointing oil, silly girl."

"What?" I asked.

Still laughing, Zena said, "Holy oil. It's designed to make you holy and everything that touches you holy."

"No, ma'am. I know what holy oil is. Trust me when I tell you that was old fish grease. I know that smell well. Now I'm going to smell like that for the rest of the day."

Zena's words were choppy and mixed with coughs and laughter. "Girl, you are too funny. I am choking."

"Whatever. Still, thank you." I appreciated how she had stepped in to ensure my day was a success. We hadn't known each other long, but she cared about me.

"You can thank me by making sure this is what you want. You are not just marrying Myles, but his family, too. And perhaps those older women. And the old fish grease."

"I know. But I do want to marry Myles." Zena didn't need to know that it had become more of an obligation than a choice.

"All right, well, let's get your makeup done and get you dressed then. You have a fine man waiting for you." She started pulling makeup from her makeup bag before she paused. "And you're sure you want your face made up like the picture you showed me?"

"I'm sure."

I closed my eyes while Zena worked her magic. For her to be nearly 50, she still had the flavor of a trendy 20-something. My mind flashed with screenshots of the finished look, and my stomach churned with anticipation.

"All done."

I leaned into the mirror, taking a closer look at Zena's magic. "I can't believe it. Girl, you have some major talent. This looks just like the picture."

"Ten minutes to showtime," Zena announced. She turned her back as I slipped into my wedding dress. When I gave her the okay, she turned around and started pulling and tugging, buttoning here and zipping there. Lastly, she placed my veil on top of my head, and I was set.

"How do I look, Zena?"

She raised her eyebrows. "Like how you wanted."

I took one last glance at Eva Moss in the antique full-body mirror that stood in the corner of the room. I was finally ready to make my grand entrance.

Entry 24

Dear Diary:

Uncle Bobby stood waiting to escort me down the aisle. His smile faded when he saw me. I only hoped it was to keep from crying. I hoped it was because he was overcome with emotion at how beautiful I was, which had rendered him speechless. He didn't say that, though. He didn't say anything. His lingering stare concerned me. I had planned to make sure he was okay, but the doors opened without warning.

From the back of the venue, I heard the gasps hit the room like gusts of wind from a hurricane. Before Uncle Bobby and I began our descent down the makeshift eighteen-foot aisle, I took a minute to reposition the long, flowing black ruffles attached to my black lace mermaid gown. Except for the V-neck cut, every part of my skin was covered. The sheer material that made up my dress's arms blended in with the sheer of my veil. The front of the veil was made of a thick black material that allowed my face to stay entirely hidden until Myles uncovered me. Zena's talent made it so that I could see out, but no one could see in.

The altar grew closer and closer. Self-talk kicked in. *Focus on the gazebo at the front of the room, Eva.*

"Finish him."

I shook my head, hoping Michael would understand now wasn't a good time. Although I was thrilled he had come, I needed to focus.

Fear, surprise, shock, disgust, and only a few smiles were plastered on the faces I passed. In my gut, I knew it was because of my dress. It had to be. I didn't remember those expressions on *Say Yes to the Dress, Four Weddings,* or even *Bridezilla* for that matter. The one thing they all had in common was traditional gowns. Then I remembered Zena's advice. *"Choose a dress that represents your personality."* And I did just that. Even if I had worn a traditional gown, someone was bound to have something negative to say.

My dress was like a shield that allowed me to muster up enough courage to be the center of attention for the day. Black represented the power I would have as soon as Myles and I exchanged vows, and the veil represented a grieving widow, who I would be as well. I was pre-mourning, in a sense. I was mourning the fact that I had to take such drastic measures to get justice for my brother. I was mourning the fact that I would soon lose my husband. I gave everyone at the wedding a warning.

It didn't matter what anyone said. I was happy because my dress represented me to the fullest. It was remarkable, current, and more my style. With that thought, confidence appeared in my walk.

When I finally rested my feet at the front, I glanced over at Mrs. Sanders. My eyes traced over her narrowed eyes and down to her parted lips.

Myles, too, had a look of concern on his face.

As the officiant gave opening remarks, Myles kept looking from me over to where his mom had sat. She wasn't in her seat anymore. I assumed she threw a tantrum of some sort because I didn't choose her dress.

"Who gives this woman to be married to this man?"

"*Me.*"

Uncle Bobby raised his hand and mumbled, "I do."

"*I do,*" Michael copied.

Myles stepped forward to take my hand. His focus was still on the empty seat where his mom had sat and now the empty seat where Sheila had sat. He could look wherever he wanted as long as he didn't leave this altar before sealing the deal.

The ceremony continued even though Mrs. Sanders had not returned to her seat. I was surprised. I thought Myles would've paused the ceremony to see what was going on with his mother.

Eventually, Mrs. Sanders and Sheila walked back in and let the doors slam. Everyone shifted their focus to the back of the church, including Myles and me. Mrs. Sanders strutted slowly back to her seat. It was like she was contemplating something. I knew I wasn't hallucinating. Not a single person in the audience remained their same hue or inhaled a single breath of air while they waited to see if she would cause a scene. My eyes burned from shooting daggers covered with fire her way as I wondered what she would do.

Myles must've had the same thoughts, because he, too, watched her as she strolled in. And he must have felt the nervous electricity flowing through my body, because he squeezed my hands tightly. "Don't look into the crowd. Look at me."

"Look at him."

This was another reason why a part of me hated what was to become his fate. He was so attentive to me and always tried to help. Sometimes I felt sorry for him. He wanted so badly to make a life with me. A good one at that. My loyalty to my brother wouldn't let me reciprocate anything positive that Myles threw my way for long.

I turned my attention back to Mrs. Sanders. She had quietly taken her seat, and the wedding went forth without any more hitches.

"You may now kiss your bride," the officiant said.

Myles smiled and rubbed his hands together, then lifted my veil. His smile vanished. A crinkle spread across his face, followed by a long pause.

"Myles and Eva sitting in a tree, k-i-s-s-i-n-g," Michael sang like when we were kids.

It wasn't until the crowd chanted, "Kiss her, kiss her," that Myles finally leaned in and pecked my black-covered lips.

"Ladies and gentlemen, I present to you Mr. and Mrs. Sanders."

The standing ovations, whistles, and loud applause faded once we turned to face the crowd.

Entry 25

Dear Diary:

The reception hall was nestled behind the Ritz and surrounded by water and various well-maintained, colorful flowers. Inside, the circular-style tables were round enough to seat everyone comfortably, and there was plenty of food, drinks, and music. I thought that once the bar opened, everyone would loosen up. Wrong. Given how beautifully the reception hall was decorated, it was a shame that the attitudes were the complete opposite. Most everyone was cold and distant toward me. I'd seen plenty of weddings, and the bride and groom were always hugged, congratulated, or something. All night, our guests barely made eye contact with me, which was entirely different from the interaction everyone had with Myles. Granted, of the two hundred guests who showed up, not even fifty belonged to me, but that didn't mean they had to ignore me.

I expected that from Mrs. Sanders and even her crew, who didn't stay long. Myles was even distant.

He hardly looked at me, and when we danced, he didn't hold me tight like he did when we danced at home. It didn't bother me until it was time for him to dance with his mother. I watched as they swayed to "A Song for Mama" by Boyz II Men. They talked and laughed throughout the entire dance. I felt like interrupting because I was his wife, and I was entitled to better treatment than Mrs. Sanders. I was supposed to be the number one Mrs. Sanders in his life.

Except for participating in the bride's responsibilities, I sat by myself much of the night. The occasional pop-ins from Zena, Clara, Uncle Bobby, and a few other people made me feel a little less invisible.

I groaned, rolled my eyes, and turned my head when the three amigos approached me.

"She married now," Uncle Buster joked.

"Congratulations," Aunt Nora's friend added.

"Yes, congrats. Beautiful ceremony, even more beautiful reception. I'm enjoying myself."

"Thanks," I hesitantly said.

"And we'd like to apologize to you for making you feel uncomfortable. We never knew you felt that way. Hopefully, you will give us a chance to make amends," Aunt Nora spoke on behalf of the nodding Uncle Buster and her friend.

"Thanks," I said again. Any chance at us reconciling wouldn't happen. I'd spent my entire life without them. I didn't need them for anything.

Boredom got the best of me. I was ready to go. My attention wavered between the present moment and later that night. Most brides anticipated the moment they would be alone with their new husband. Not me. The idea of consummating the marriage wasn't exciting. It was the idea of what I wanted to do to him. I was excited about straddling him as he slept. Again, not for consummation. I looked forward to placing a pillow over his face, keeping his neck visible while I added more and more pressure until I could see the veins pop out of his neck as he struggled to breathe. I'd consider it a wedding gift to myself.

"Hey, hey." Tipsy Sheila held the mic. She rocked and stumbled, which was surprising because, with the way she turned her nose up at me, I would have sworn she was perfect. "I think I had a little too much to drink."

"Me too," Myles shouted. "Just tonight. It won't happen again," he said and guzzled straight from a liquor bottle.

I gasped. He'd relapsed. All that progress down the drain.

Sheila laughed and hiccupped. "We have lanterns. Get to the lake."

My interest was piqued. I didn't have to wait until tonight. I could handle Myles at the lake. It was dark. He couldn't swim. I could push him in. No one would suspect a thing.

"Finish him."

I would.

Our guests huddled around us with their lanterns. As each person released one, they spoke
sweet sentiments, words of wisdom, and advice. I
listened for the opportune moment to push him
in. I picked up on the pattern. All eyes were on
the person speaking, and when they looked up,
everyone looked up.

Our positioning was perfect. Myles stood behind
me, closer to the edge, with his hands wrapped
around my waist. Quite surprising since he'd been
distant toward me most of the night. When he
kissed my cheek, neck, and earlobe, I could smell
the alcohol on his breath. That was a big help.

I rehearsed the believable explanation I'd give
when the cops and divers finally pulled his body
from the water. *"He had too much to drink and
stepped off the edge of the dock, Officers. We tried
to save him, but it was too dark to reach him."*

Perhaps he'd get tangled with the plant life
underneath or eaten by an alligator.

Sweet sentiments. Words of wisdom. Advice.
Everyone looked up. It was like clockwork.

Next speech, I'd bump him into the water.

Sweet sentiments. Words of wisdom. Advice.
Everyone looked up. I tried to take a step back,
but my feet wouldn't move. It was like slabs of
concrete weighed them down.

"Finish him."

Sweet sentiments. Words of wisdom. Advice. Everyone looked up.

"It's beautiful, isn't it? The way the moon glistens over the water," Myles whispered in my ear.

"Do it."

Sweet sentiments. Words of wisdom. Advice. Everyone looked up.

This time my feet felt weightless.

"Push."

Sweet sentiments. Words of wisdom. Advice.

No one looked up. They all looked around and applauded.

That was it. That was all the lanterns.

Everyone dispersed back inside. I missed the opportunity. *Tonight for sure.*

Myles seemed to be into me before we left the reception and headed upstairs to the honeymoon suite. We posed for a couple of pictures together and even shared a few kisses. The chemistry from Myles seemed to fade once we were alone. And yet they said I was the one with a mood disorder.

At the door of the suite, I expected him to carry me over the threshold as I'd seen on TV, but instead, he unlocked the door and stepped to the side, motioning for me to enter. I entered the room using my own two feet as he followed me. I stood beside the bed, thinking he would approach me from behind with affection. Maybe even unzip my dress. That didn't happen either. He walked around me. Then he loosened his tie, grabbed the remote, and plopped down in the recliner, where ESPN held his attention.

His attitude toward me was unusual. I wondered if he had already begun to doubt his choice of bride. Or maybe it was all the liquor he consumed. I'd never seen him drunk before. I tried small talk. "If you don't want to be with me, then why did you go through with tonight?"

He sat stone-faced.

"Do you wish you could have married Sabrina instead of me? Or even that officer?"

He frowned and aggressively rubbed his temples as though he were trying to remove the questions from his memory bank. "So we are going to do this on our wedding night?"

"It doesn't seem like much of a wedding night when you are barely saying anything to me."

"It's hard to say anything to you like this." He made an up-and-down movement with his hand.

"Like what? Am I not beautiful to you?"

"Honestly? And I don't want to hurt your feelings, but you asked. What is with all the black? The black dress. The black makeup. The black lipstick. The black nail polish. The black raccoon circles around your eyes. I don't get it."

I quoted Zena by telling him how I wanted my wedding gown and makeup to reflect my personality, not someone else's.

"The least you could've done was tell my mother that you had changed your mind on wearing her dress. Hell, why not prepare me? Why not tell me you wanted to do something unorthodox?"

"Sympathize."

"Myles, I'm sorry. It's just that I didn't like your mom's dress. It wasn't my style. She pushed herself on me, and I didn't get a chance to object. I knew how important it was to her, and I didn't have the heart to tell her. I hoped that what I chose would make her happy enough to forget that I was even supposed to wear her gown."

At least Myles looked at me.

"More."

"When I took the dress in for alterations, Zena helped me to realize that it was my day—"

"Our day," Myles corrected me.

"Our day," I repeated. "Zena helped me to realize that it was *our* day and that my dress needed to reflect my personality."

Myles nodded before saying, "I get that. I understand everything you've said, but since when did the gothic look become you? Who shows up to their wedding looking like Marilyn Manson other than Marilyn Manson?"

"Cry."

I couldn't do that on cue. I inched over to Myles, who was still seated in the recliner, and rested my palms on his knees. "Myles, I know you're upset, but please understand why I did what I did. Other than my aunt and uncle, you are all the family I have, and I didn't want to be unhappy, nor did I mean to offend anyone. I'm sorry, and I understand if you need space. All my life, I've been treated differently, like an outcast—which is just how goths are treated—and that's what I felt best represented me. But I can understand how I should have communicated that with you because it was your day as well."

Myles pulled me up into his lap. "I love you, Eva, but please go and wash all that black junk off of your face."

Michael had coached me through, and it worked.

I smiled and did as Myles requested. Since I had to time Operation Pillow right, I carried on with the night as an ordinary bride would. Zena had gifted me with some fiery red lace lingerie to wear. When I returned from the bathroom and allowed Myles to see me in lingerie for the first time, ESPN was no longer his focus. He was undressed before he made the five steps over to me.

That night of my wedding was the first time Myles and I connected sexually, and it made me think twice about doing anything to hurt him.

Entry 26

Dear Diary:

Because sex with Myles felt so good, I had encouraged myself to resume taking my medication. I was having fun, walking around with a sore vagina and all. A good sore, though. I wanted to give being a wife a fair shot. However, Michael felt differently. *"Stop all medication,"* he had instructed.

I had never been more torn in my life. I heard Michael, but Myles and I humped like rabbits, and every time we finished our bedroom activities, I promised I'd let him live one more day so we could do it one more time, and then I'd be satisfied enough to take care of him like Michael wanted.

I began to wonder why I waited so long to feel the touch of a man. He was so gentle and patient with me that I considered fully surrendering to the medication regime and choosing Myles over Michael because I wasn't ready to let go of the euphoria.

Michael wanted one thing, and Myles wanted another. Two totally different spectrums. I *think*

I knew what I wanted. The only thing I didn't know was how to make the *three* of us happy. To make Michael happy, I needed to hurt Myles. To make Myles happy, I needed to be consistent with medication and therapy. To make myself happy, I wanted to have both my brother and my husband in my life. Peacefully.

Though I had found a way to balance Michael and Myles, I still yearned for an ordinary life instead of one where I had to perform balancing acts.

I was current on my shot, but I wasn't taking my oral meds. Michael instructed me to take the pills once every three days. Myles wanted me to take them like Dr. Monroe prescribed, every day, faithfully. I did my own thing and divided their desires. One every other day. The nausea was unbearable, and the aches pounded against my head harder than my heart pounded against my chest. Essentially, I realized that I didn't have things under control like I had thought.

I needed to make a final decision and stick with it.

I thought back to the questions asked during our premarital counseling sessions. "In what order would you place your family members based on the level of importance to you?" Then we were asked a similar but reversed question. "In what order do you think your partner's level of importance should be compared to where you think it is right now?"

We were told not to answer but to only reflect on it. From there, we were given two single worksheets that had those very same questions on them. The box below had listings for mother, father, siblings, grandparents, and so on. We were not to discuss our answers until we returned.

I happened to "stumble" across Myles's worksheet while he was at work. There was something about his top drawer that revealed the most exciting things. I ran to my room to get my worksheet. I laid them side by side. My eyes shifted from right to left, then left to right as I made comparisons. His answers were completely different from mine. My name was in a place where I didn't expect it to be. Then I wondered if I should change my answers to match his. Because according to what I was looking at, we wouldn't make it as a couple. We would barely make it as roommates.

Good thing I wrote in pencil.

"I see that you both are united when it comes to how you would rank each other." The counselor had smiled. "Not too many couples understand the importance of no longer viewing their parents or other family members as a top priority. Some couples face lots of trouble within their marriage, even resulting in divorce, when they don't place their spouse first. You two share the same beliefs. You're both a priority in your union, and everyone comes after. I am impressed."

Myles had squeezed my hand. I assumed it was to say he was relieved and happy with the results.

I had smiled at the fact that I was smart enough to flip that pencil over and erase every shred of evidence showing where I ranked Myles well after Michael. To be honest, I ranked Zena before him, too.

Thinking back on that exercise, I decided that I would give Myles a fair chance. One hundred percent. But before I could commit to that and commit to taking full advantage of therapy, I felt I owed it to Michael to have that conversation with him. In doing so, I hoped the current plan would be revised to satisfy all parties.

Things didn't go according to plan. Michael had been quiet. I felt it was because I had disobeyed him, and he felt a need to punish me. A light bulb went off. Decrease the dosage like he had suggested, and all would be forgiven, at least long enough for me to tell my brother about the life I wanted to explore.

Marriage was growing increasingly intriguing to me by the day. Myles and I had formed a strong bond, like the unbreakable bond that he and Michael shared before the accident. We were in a good place.

"Sweetness," Myles said. That was how he usually addressed me when he had something up his sleeve or when he wanted me to get naked.

I batted my lashes and started taking off my top.

"Whoa." He laughed. "I was actually coming to talk to you about something."

"Oh." I felt stupid.

"Since you started undressing, go ahead and finish. I can watch and talk."

I did without hesitation. By the time he opened his mouth, I was naked.

"My agency is throwing a Christmas party, and I wanted to know if you'd be interested in going."

Every inch of me smiled. "Really? I get to go to your place of work?"

"Yeah, why not? You have never been, and it would be nice to show off all this."

"I just figured you didn't want me around them or something. Especially since none of them were invited to the wedding. I thought you were ashamed of me."

Myles frowned and wrapped my naked body in his arms. "As beautiful as you are, there is nothing for me to be ashamed of."

"But I'm 'crazy.'" I made air quotes.

"I like them a little 'crazy,'" he joked, making air quotes of his own. "After Sabrina, I prefer to keep my personal life private."

"What does that mean?" I asked, hoping to hear that something was wrong with Sabrina like there was with me.

"The wives are very cliquey and gave her a hard time. I don't want them trying to bully you or force you to join the petty wives club."

"The petty wives club? Is that a real thing?"

Myles smacked his teeth. "Eva, no," he laughed. "I call them that because they hang around the office a lot and keep up drama. They turn their noses up at the new wives and girlfriends or try to intimidate them."

I nodded. "Good thing I'm a loner. Besides, all I need is you." I wiggled my breasts to seduce him, but he kept talking about work.

"Yeah, but I have seen them and how overbearing they can be. Most of them are stay-at-home moms who frequently volunteer at their kids' schools, carpool, and sponsor fundraisers. Well, except Joan, the meanest one, the pack leader. She does something in the medical field at a hospital or something." He shrugged. "I just don't want you to feel pressured by them."

"No worries. Those are things I'd never see myself doing. And we already agreed that we wouldn't have any children, so that eliminates me from their clique."

The topic of children had come up, but because mental illness can be hereditary, we decided against it. If we changed our minds, adoption was an option.

"They are going to try to get under your skin, especially Joan. She's still upset that I beat out her husband as lead agent. She made some comments saying they only hired me to have a black person in a management position."

"I can handle it. I can handle the party. I can handle the crowd. And I can handle those wives."

Entry 27

Dear Diary:

I learned a little something from my engagement party—dress to impress. And since I would be among snobbish, judgmental women who were fascinated with labels and statuses, I made sure to look my best. I would have asked Zena to make me a one-of-a-kind piece, but there wasn't enough time with the party being three days away. So I got some ideas from binge-watching the reality shows that I'd become addicted to. This time I studied each lady's style and technique.

Since I was in Georgia, I wanted to emulate the ladies of Georgia. With my computer on my lap, a notebook, pen, and remote in hand, I scrolled through the DVR before deciding on *The Real Housewives of Atlanta*. I paid close attention to their outfits, the way they spoke, and even down to the way they held their peach during their opening introductions.

My notebook was full of ideas. But to be safe, I needed more. I then flipped over to *Married to*

Medicine and took more notes. By the time I finished, my black-and-white composition notebook had only a few empty pages left.

After studying my notes and surfing the web, I found what I needed. Neiman Marcus had the perfect asymmetrical Versace dress that retailed for $2,495. Before I bought it, I did the right thing. I got naked and approached my husband. I wasn't much of a dancer, but he found me twerking when he looked up from his computer.

Although he was working, he set his computer to the side to take in the performance. "Damn, babe. Wait, let me get my wallet." When Myles returned, he said, "Okay, resume."

I assumed he liked the show. He smacked my jiggling cakes, reached in his wallet, and made it rain. I appreciated it, but I needed a lot more money than that. I was out of breath and sweaty when I plopped on his lap.

"Encore," Myles said.

I was tired. I had instant admiration for strippers. Dancing seductively required skill and stamina. I had neither, but at least it was enough to make my husband's mini me excited.

I pinched my fingers together. "I need a tiny favor."

Myles shook his head. "I should've known all this was for a reason. What's up, Parkay?"

Confusion mixed with sweat and ran down my face.

Myles snickered and then burst into an uncontrollable laugh.

I went to walk away, but he pulled me back into his lap and started tickling me. "I'm teasing, baby. What's up?"

"Who is Parkay?"

"It's margarine, baby. It was a joke."

"I don't get it."

"I see," Myles said before laughing again. "Parkay is margarine. Like butter. You danced to butter me up because you want something. So that's why I called you Parkay."

It took a second before the elevator reached the top floor with the ding and all. I let out a long, exaggerated, "Ohhhhhh."

We started wrestling when I pinched him over that dad joke. I loved fun moments like this because even I knew how uptight and serious I could be.

Once playtime settled down, I jumped right into the request. "There's a dress I'd like to buy for the party. It's expensive, so I wanted to make sure it was okay with you first."

"Can I at least see it first? I've seen the dresses you pick."

That statement sent us both into a fit of laughter. That, too, felt good. Just as it had since we'd mar-

ried. Something about us becoming one caused m
to look at him differently. At times I struggled, bu
the scale tipped more toward me wanting to mak
things work with him.

"Impressive. I like that, babe. Go ahead and ge
it."

"Do you want to know how much it is first?"

He shook his head. "Not really. Get what yo
like."

A part of me wanted to leave it there, but h
needed to know. "It's twenty-four hundred dollars
I said and pursed my lips.

"Okay," Myles said without wincing. "Put it o
your credit card."

"Are you sure it's not too much?"

"It might be, but since you got me all riled up an
are naked, sit on it, and I'll overlook the price."

"Myles Sanders, you are trying to turn your wi
into a prostitute."

He shrugged. "I don't see anything wrong wit
it. I like 'em nasty." He licked his juicy lips.

"And crazy, according to you."

"Hey. At least I'm honest." Myles's eyes fille
with even more lust, making me become his pro
titute.

I became his nasty girl again before the part
The dress fit my body like a glove. I got all dolle
up, and thanks to the mobile makeup artist, th
only thing on me that was black was my ligh

eyeliner. I walked with my head up, proud to be
Eva Ann Moss-Sanders.

Myles was all over me. I had never turned him
down when he wanted sex, but I pushed him back.
I don't feel good."

That didn't stop him. He was back on me. "I can
make you feel better in two minutes if you let me."

I loved his sexual innuendos. I turned around
and lifted my dress.

"This dress looks way better on you than it did
on the model," he said to me and inserted himself.
He didn't lie. He had me feeling better within two
minutes. That was just the first round. The second
and third rounds were much longer and more
satisfying.

Needless to say, we were late for the party. I was
surprised we made it at all. He gave me three good
rounds, and I gave him round four in the car.

Inside the venue, I immediately spotted the
clique. They all stood together, stiff and plastic
looking. Must have been their Botox injections in
preparation for tonight. I couldn't wait to meet
them. I leaned over to Myles. "Are any of those human mannequins standing by the staircase Joan?"

Myles glanced in their direction. "Yes, that's her
in the white dress."

Joan was basic. Especially the dress she had on.
I'd done my fair share of bargain shopping, and
that was a bargain.

Myles and I stood in the same spot for nearly an hour, and none of the plastic ladies bothered to introduce themselves or congratulate us on our wedding. Each time I looked in their direction, they tooted their noses up. I, in turn, rolled my eyes.

Silverware hitting against a glass silenced everyone, and then came a long toast. I pretended to pay attention, but my focus was still on Joan. The arrows pointing to the corner behind the staircase served as my exit.

My patience had weakened. "I'm going to the ladies' room," I told Myles.

"Do you want me to go with you?" he asked.

Laughing, I said, "I can go by myself. Ain't no telling what you'll try to do to me if you get me alone again." Really, I wanted to get near Joan to teach her a thing or two about messing with my man. If anyone was going to be mean to him, it was me and only me.

Myles grinned and held up his glass of water in agreement. "Facts."

I made heavy eye contact as I strutted past the ladies. One blew a kiss at me, one frowned, and everyone else smirked.

As I adjusted my dress and hair in the mirror, one of the cliquey ladies entered the bathroom looking even more basic. She stood in the mirror pretending to powder her nose, but I could tell she was there to spy on me. No words were exchanged, just glares.

I made eye contact again as I returned to Myles's side. He was surrounded by Joan's husband, Roger, and some other men. When Roger kissed the back of my hand, Joan hurried over. Judging by how fast she got there, I swear she could have won a gold medal in the Olympics.

"Honey, this is an amazing party," she said, ignoring Myles and me.

"Joan, meet Eva," Roger said. "And you know Myles."

"Myles." She nodded and then turned her attention to me. "You look so familiar. Have we met before?"

"I don't believe so," I said. I extended my left hand with a flick so she'd notice the massive wedding ring that I wore compared to her simple gold band. "It's a pleasure to meet you, Joan."

"I didn't know Myles was in a serious relationship," she said as she admired my ring. "Anytime I am around the office, he's never mentioned you." The phony smile she gave caused her eyes to squint.

"Well, now you know. And although I'm sure you will, please share the good news with everyone else who may not know of me." I followed up with a phony smile of my own.

She calmed down for a moment, leading me to believe the battle was over. As soon as the tension within me eased, she spewed more venom.

"Myles, I thought you and Maria were still fooling around."

It all happened so fast. Roger said something inaudible to Joan. My head swung over to Myles, and I noticed several wrinkles in his forehead. The noise level in our huddle turned down several notches.

"Maria?" I repeated. Myles had warned me of how vicious and territorial Joan was, but he failed to inform me of Maria.

The look on Joan's face said that she was about to finish me off. And she did. "You've never met Maria when you've come to the office?" Joan smirked and sipped from her wineglass.

The wrinkles in Myles's forehead deepened. "Roger, man, get your wife under control. What the hell is she talking about?"

"Joan, that's enough," Roger interjected. "Myles and Eva, please accept my sincerest apologies. I think maybe my wife has had way too much to drink." He yanked Joan's wrist and led her away.

And just like that, Joan managed to diminish every ounce of self-confidence that I had. She got the best of me. My issue was no longer with her. Myles tried to make her out to be a witch to cover up his bad behavior.

"Who is Maria?" I demanded to know.

I knew it would be a lousy night for Myles because the minute he touched my shoulder, I jerked away. "Joan is drunk. Don't pay her any attention. I told you, she's an evil, bitter woman."

"Is she? Or do you feel that way because she calls you out on your women?" I barked. "Don't deny it, Myles. Why would she just make up something so random?"

"Baby, I promise you there is no Maria."

I pointed around the room. "Which one is she? Just tell me."

"Let's not do this here, please."

"Why not? Is this where you do Maria?"

"Do not make a scene. We can talk in private. Now let's go."

"I'm not leaving until I find Maria."

"Eva, there is no Maria."

"Oh, so you're gonna try to make it like I'm imagining this too?" I shook my head, then yelled, "Who is Maria? Maria, show yourself."

"Eva, stop it." Myles pulled me over to Roger, who stood near the bar looking nervous while guzzling down drinks. Joan was right by his side.

"As a man, it would be disrespectful of me to address your wife, so I'm going to say this to you. What the hell is wrong with her? And what the hell is wrong with you? You stand by and watch her treat people like this all the time. Where are your balls, man? Or does your wife own them?"

Roger stumbled over his words. "I . . . I . . . I can fix this."

Myles stepped in his face. "It needs to be fixed now."

Roger nodded and turned to Joan, motioning for her to say something. She was hesitant to speak, so he yelled at her. She then said the most disgusting thing. "Don't take it out on me because your wife is bat-shit crazy."

The party turned into pure chaos. It took a swarm of people to hold Myles back.

I was humiliated. How would Joan know that, unless . . . "You told them about me, Myles? How would she know that?"

"I didn't tell them shit." Something clicked in Myles's brain. "What hospital does Joan work at?" Myles asked one of the guys trying to calm him down.

"I'm not sure," the guy answered.

"That information is very important. I have one grand in my pocket for you if you can find out."

"On it. I can ask my girl. She hung out with them awhile before she declared them mean girls."

"Thank you," Myles said. He reached in his wallet and pulled out a wad of cash that he didn't bother to count. "Down payment. Eva, let's go."

I didn't want to go with Myles, nor did I want to stay at this party. I picked what I thought was the lesser of two evils and followed Myles out the door.

Roger ran alongside us, apologizing and promising to get his wife under control.

I had never seen Myles so angry. He became even more upset when his phone rang. It was the man he paid.

"I appreciate you. I owe you." Myles fumed and mumbled threats.

"What did he say?" I asked.

"Why do you care? It's not like you'll believe me anyway," he snapped at me.

"You can't get mad at me because you got caught cheating."

"Fuck!" Myles yelled and punched the steering wheel.

That was one of my moves. He seriously needed to get checked out. As a matter of fact, I was willing to give him the medication that I wasn't taking.

"Are you okay?" I asked. When I touched him, he yanked away from me this time.

"Please don't touch me, Eva."

"Why are you upset with me?"

"Because you are always doing stuff to humiliate me. It's one thing when it's just me. I can handle it better than I can when it happens in front of my family and colleagues. And all for nothing."

"But Joan started it."

"Yeah, she may have started it, but at what point do you trust me? When I tell you it's nothing, believe that for a change."

"Men always lie, and you had no business telling her about my health challenges."

Myles scoffed and nodded. "Okay, Eva. I hate to burst your bubble, but remember when I told you Joan worked at a hospital? She works at Piedmont Psychiatric Hospital. The place I took you to when the Sabrina incident happened. Joan is the discharge coordinator, and I'm assuming when your chart came across her desk for review, she saw my name. Because of her bitterness, ego, and fear of losing her coveted position as 'lead wife' since her husband is not the lead agent, she decided to have a little fun with your mind."

"She can't do that. That's a violation of her job."

"Well, she did, and instead of trusting me, you fell for it. So hear me clearly. Maria does not exist. She was only a trigger to induce your paranoia."

"She can get fired for that."

"I'm sure Joan will find a way to spin it. You should have trusted me."

"Well, next time I will."

"I don't think there will be a next time."

"What is that supposed to mean?"

"I need time. I need time to think if I want to continue to put up with this."

My heart seemed to break into tiny pieces. Pieces that were too small to put back together. "You're leaving?"

He blew out a long breath before saying, "I just need some space right now."

With all his efforts to prepare me for the function, things still went wrong. I thought I could handle it.

"Myles, you can't leave me. I'm pregnant."

Entry 28

Dear Diary:

Three months had passed since I announced my pregnancy to Myles. He didn't leave me, but there was an uncomfortable shift in our relationship. He moved out of the bedroom he shared with me and into the spare room, and no matter how many times I appeared naked in front of him or tried to get physical, I was invisible to him.

The night Myles threatened to leave me, it made me nervous. It made me want to get my act together. I made sure that I was current on my shot, and I began taking my oral meds as prescribed.

Faithfully.

Myles was not attentive to my pregnancy needs. Plus, he was dry and distant as a husband. Fun times for us were long gone. Whenever I'd try to make small talk, Myles would offer only a few words in return.

He did manage to ask the same question often. "How did you become pregnant if you're on birth control?"

"Abstinence is the only guaranteed method," I told him.

"Uh-huh."

"You should know that." I rolled my eyes, not happy with his line of questioning.

No matter how much I tried to be a doting wife and make the best of the situation, there was always some kind of question from Myles. The more he inquired, the more difficult the questions became.

As I made dinner one night, Myles decided to interrogate me, which was nothing new lately. "How many months along did you say you were?"

"Three."

"Three?" he repeated. "Why is your stomach still flat? And I could have sworn I've seen period pads in your trash can."

"Yes, three. And the sanitary napkins are being used for something associated with my pregnancy, not my cycle."

He cocked his head to the side and poked out his lips to question the validity of my statement.

To further prove him wrong, I untied my apron and lifted my shirt to show him that my stomach was growing. "Remember, Myles, you and I have not been together as husband and wife since the day of your Christmas party, so you have no idea what my body looks like." I then cocked my head to the side and poked out my lips as a way of saying, "Checkmate."

That still wasn't enough for him. "Make sure you let me know when the next appointment is."

"For what?" I asked. "Ever since I announced the pregnancy, you've been unavailable. It's been three months, and not once have you asked me how I'm doing, how I'm feeling, nothing other than how it happened."

"I haven't asked you anything because I don't believe you or anything you say."

"That's silly. Why would I make this up?"

"That's what I'm trying to figure out," Myles said. "When was the last time you took your injection?"

"At my last visit a couple of weeks ago," I said matter-of-factly. "Why are you so concerned all of a sudden? You stopped coming to appointments with me, remember?"

"Yeah, I do. That's because you were stable enough to get yourself there and back."

"And I can still manage to get myself there and back. So don't concern yourself with what's going on with me, my pregnancy, or my child."

He let out a chuckle and walked over to his work area. He pulled out a book along with a brown paper bag. He held on to the bag but tossed the book in my direction. It landed close enough to me to see the title written in big letters.

"And you're trying to make what point with this book, Myles?"

He shook his head in disbelief. "I did a little research, and if you're really pregnant, then you would no longer be on an injection because it is harmful to the fetus."

I peered at the book again. "Just because you ran out and purchased a book on managing mental health and pregnancy doesn't make you an expert. Dr. Monroe and my ob-gyn have discussed my current condition and felt it was better to keep me on the injection than it was to take me off."

He started to walk off but stopped. "What is the name of your ob-gyn?"

"Dr. None of Your Business," I answered.

"As the father, I have a right to know and a right to be present for those conversations, especially when it concerns the health of my child. So again, let me know when the next appointment is."

"I'm not telling you anything other than when to show up for the delivery. *If* I decide to have you there."

He pulled out his phone and dialed a number. Because he had it on speaker, I heard, "Dr. Monroe's office. This is Amber. How can I help you?"

"What are you doing?" I asked. Little did he know there would be a surprise waiting for him on the receiving end of that call.

"This is Myles Sanders. I am Eva Sanders's husband. Well, I'm not sure if she's listed as Moss or

Sanders, but I am calling to make an appointment for us to come in and speak with Dr. Monroe regarding a substitution for her injection since she's pregnant."

"I don't need an appointment, Amber. I already know what's going on." I said from the background.

"One moment, please," Amber said and placed Myles on hold.

I leaned my back against the sink, listening to the hold music with my arms folded across my chest because I knew he wouldn't be able to obtain any information.

When Amber returned, she said, "Unfortunately, Mr. Sanders, we will need a release of information to discuss anything with you."

"I signed one already when we first came into the office."

"I understand, but it has since been rescinded."

"Rescinded?" Myles asked.

"I'm afraid so," she said.

"I'm afraid so," I repeated. I removed that paper that granted release of my medical information to Myles. I was one step ahead, and since he acted like he didn't care, there was no reason for him to have access to anything concerning me.

That poor receptionist. Myles didn't say bye or anything. He just hung up.

"Here, take this." Myles held out the brown paper bag.

I looked inside and laughed. "A pregnancy test? Really?" I tossed the bag on the counter.

"Just so I understand, you say you're pregnant, but you are refusing to take the test that I have here for you?"

"You understand really well. I'm not taking it."

"Okay, cool. Since you refuse to take the test and keep me in the loop with what's going on, I will not do anything for the *alleged* baby until it's born. I want a DNA test, too."

I hated it when he threatened to leave me. "Leaving is not necessary. You are being silly."

He pointed to the bag. "Are you going to take the test or not?"

"Are you hard of hearing? I already told you no."

"I'm out. I'll take what I can now and come back to get the rest of my things." Myles turned to walk away.

Threats bothered me, and Myles had threatened me again. I couldn't handle another person leaving me. He was just mad. I thought that once I finished cooking, he'd sit down and eat with me like we used to do. Then we'd have a conversation, he would calm down, and we'd be okay.

Even though I was preparing another twenty-minute meal that I'd found online this time, those twenty minutes were moving at a turtle's pace. I wanted to sit and talk with Myles over dinner, maybe convince him to stay, but at the rate he used to pack, I wasn't sure if the food would be done in time. He had two suitcases lined against the sofa and a gym bag sitting on the floor. He disappeared into his room again. When he came out this time, his arms were filled with clothes. It didn't seem like he planned to come back.

I took slow, deep breaths, but the nervousness caused my entire body to shiver. I was going to run out of time. I looked at the chicken and back at Myles. He threw a bag over his shoulder.

I needed to gauge how much time I had, so I asked, "Myles, will you at least stay for dinner? It's almost ready."

He rolled his suitcases near the door. "Nah, I'm good."

"I was hoping that we could have dinner together and talk."

"There isn't much to talk about at this point."

"We are married, Myles. Remember in counseling she said we had to work through our problems?" I tried my best to guilt him.

He snapped, "Yeah, but our problems can't be worked through."

"Myles, please, I am begging you. Can we please sit and talk? Please."

By this time, he had all his bags at the door. A gym bag rested on top of two large suitcases, and he was going back for something else.

He's really leaving. "I never knew Myles Sanders was capable of leaving his pregnant wife alone."

"And I never knew my wife would lie about being pregnant."

"You're a coward. Things get tough, and you leave me and your unborn child. What if something happens? This is not safe."

He looked around the loft. "Look where you live. There is security all around. You'll be fine."

"Security cannot help me if something goes wrong with my health while I'm carrying this child."

Myles cleared his throat. "Yeah, okay. I'll call you sometime this week and provide you with my attorney's information. Anything that needs to be said concerning the baby can go through them."

I was miffed. "What do I need to talk to an attorney for?"

"This marriage just isn't for me," he said.

"You can't leave me. I'm having a baby. Your baby."

Myles dropped his bags, walked over to the counter, and picked up the pregnancy test. "Okay, all I am asking you to do is pee on this stick, and I'm good." He held it out for me to take it.

I didn't take it. I instead threatened him. "If you walk out that door, I'll kill myself."

"I would hope not, but that's your choice."

I was shocked at his lack of compassion.

"I have dealt with your episodes. I have dealt with your mood swings and seeing people who aren't there. I am not going to stand here and allow you to control me by threatening suicide."

"The only person I've seen who was not there was Sabrina, so don't say 'people.'"

Myles frowned. "You're forgetting one. Michael."

"If Michael is dead, prove it. Show me his obituary like you showed me Sabrina's."

"If he's alive, then you prove that he is," Myles argued.

When I didn't move or say anything, he asked, "Are you gonna take the test or not?"

"Not."

"That's because you're lying, Eva. I'm giving you the opportunity to prove to me that you are pregnant. If you're lying, I am giving you the opportunity to admit to your lies. It's that simple."

"Why are you doing this, Myles? Are you in love with someone else?"

He sighed. "Don't start that shit again, trying to flip it on me because I caught you in lies."

I made another attempt to persuade him not to leave. "I'll take the test after we talk over dinner."

"You are crazy as hell if you think I am about to listen to another lie," he said and turned to walk out of the kitchen.

Myles referring to me as crazy triggered something within me, and I reacted without thinking.

The cast-iron skillet that sat on the stove with high flames rising underneath caught my attention. I grabbed it and smashed it against his head. He dropped to the floor. I hovered over him, waiting for him to get up, but he didn't.

Entry 29

Dear Diary:

There came that sound at the door that I had anticipated for a week: three bangs, then silence. In that moment of stillness, I thought maybe I was getting worked up for nothing.

"Police!"

Maybe I wasn't.

After my last phone conversation with Mrs. Sanders, I suspected the cops wouldn't be too far behind. She had called Myles several times over several days, and because he couldn't answer, she began to call me.

"He's not here," I told her, which technically wasn't a lie. He was here but not here. Here physically but definitely not in spirit.

"When will he be back?" she pried. "It's not like him not to call me or at least return any of my calls."

She was getting on my last nerve. I could see why most married people wanted to get rid of their mothers-in-law. "He's just busy. He's gotten quite a few new clients. I haven't talked to him much either."

"That's never stopped him from touching base with me before," she snapped. "Well, when you hear from him, please tell him to call me. I am starting to worry."

"Yes, ma'am. As soon as he walks through the door, I will have him call you."

Did I care about soothing her concerns? Absolutely not, but I would say anything to relieve the pressure she had placed on me. She was pushy and controlling. Back when Myles and I were kids, I only encountered her during school functions, and even then, she held a tight rein on Myles. Anytime he walked from her side, she gave him the stank eye. That look was so deadly that he retreated almost every time. I was surprised he could hang out away from home as much as he did. The most Mrs. Sanders and I said to one another were "hi" and "bye." It seemed like anytime we were in one another's presence, she always tooted her nose up at me. Far different from when we started dating. She was a lot more welcoming.

Shortly after I hung up the phone with her, she called again. "Do you know why his phone is going straight to voicemail?" Mrs. Sanders asked.

"Maybe a meeting."

"Very well. Have him call me." She was abrupt, ending the call without warning,

Why couldn't she just accept what I told her and leave it alone like his job did? Being his wife, I was listed as the emergency contact. When they called to inquire about Myles's whereabouts, my response was simple. "I am so sorry. I was supposed to call to let you know that Myles is sick. I've been so focused on taking care of him that I forgot to call."

They accepted what I said and wished him a speedy recovery.

But because Mrs. Sanders was pushy, she sent the cops to my door to perform a welfare check.

Was there a customary rule that required officers to bang precisely three times? Because they did it again, three loud bangs. "Police," they called out once more.

The rhythm of my heartbeat changed.

I paced.

I panicked.

I paced some more. "Think, Eva, think," I said aloud, but in a whisper so the police wouldn't hear me.

My stupid brain wasn't working. It wouldn't think.

I panicked some more.

The breathing techniques that I learned in therapy were pointless. I couldn't take in enough air. I couldn't risk removing the surgical mask I'd worn to rid my nose of the stench of Myles's decaying body that lay in the spare bedroom that he moved back into months ago to escape me. I had thought about dumping his lifeless body before anyone noticed, but he was too heavy, and our building was heavily guarded. I struggled just dragging his limp body into the guest room so I didn't have to look at him. Or smell him as much.

The police officers knocked again. Working under pressure was not my strong suit, but I had to do something. I'd remain quiet until they believed no one was home, and then I'd dismember Myles and haul his body off in small sections. Security would never suspect a thing.

I blamed him for what happened. Had he swallowed his skepticism and trusted me, things would have turned out differently.

I tiptoed throughout the house, grabbing large suitcases and duffel bags. There was a loud thud, almost like a bomb had gone off. The cops had entered using a battering ram. I didn't see that coming. I thought if I pretended not to be home, they'd leave.

They saw me standing in the middle of the floor holding a butcher knife. The layout of the loft left very few hiding spaces. With nowhere to run, I held the knife to my neck. This wasn't the way I wanted to go. If it were up to me, I would swallow an abundance of pills. What I had was plenty of pills but not plenty of time. They'd simply force it out of my system like before.

We had a stare-off. Me versus the multiple guns pointing at me.

"Put the knife down!" the officers yelled. "Put the knife down or we will shoot."

That didn't seem like a bad idea.

The more they yelled, the closer they inched to me.

The short standoff, filled with commands for me to put the knife down, exhausted me. I gave up and did as I was instructed.

During the roughness of them trying to cuff me, my mask repositioned. I would never forget how strong that stench had grown since the first day I got a whiff. The odor latched on to my nose hairs, making a permanent residence the same way the hospital smell did. Only with this odor, my stomach churned, and my eyes watered. Even with a mask, I could still smell a rotting corpse.

A few days after I had dragged his body to his room, I decided to peek in on him just in case anything changed. I never checked for a pulse. Just maybe I had knocked him unconscious. It was an unsettling sight. His eyes were wide open. Rigor mortis had settled in. His body was bloated, smelly, and covered with insects, and liquid poured from his mouth. I wished I had never walked in there to see that.

As I sat, waiting to be escorted out, I watched as the officers searched my home. I saw one officer twist the knob to the door where Myles was. I warned him, "I wouldn't do that if I were you." I couldn't imagine anyone, not even the coroner, getting through that without vomiting a time or two. I had vomited. That was still in there, too.

"Why shouldn't we look in there?" another officer asked.

I gave a one-shoulder shrug.

"We are going to find out what's behind that door. We can already smell it." He knelt in front of me, making eye contact. "Help us and help yourself. Just tell us so we can be prepared."

His voice faded out as my focus turned to Myles's room. The officers rubbed some type of salve under their noses before entering. The large, well-positioned white letters that spelled out POLICE on the back of the officers' jackets were now stretched and uneven as they attempted to use them as additional nose guards.

I warned them. Plus, I was sick. Sick people like me didn't go to jail. I'd do a little extended stint in the hospital and go home. But then the unexpected happened. The officers raised me from my seated position. "You have the right to remain silent. Anything you say can, and will, be used against you in a court of law . . ."

When the officer finished reading me my rights, I asked, "If I am going to the hospital, why are you reading me my rights?"

"You're being placed under arrest."

"Oh, no, people like me don't go to jail." My feet stopped moving. The more they pulled and pushed me to walk, the more weight I placed on my knees. With a jerk of my shoulders to the left and right, I managed to break free. An officer grabbed me by the back of my neck and threw me to the ground, where I suffered a few scrapes and bruises that required medical attention.

It was an unordinary ER visit. Usually, I would have to wait for hours before being seen. This time I was a priority and even had my own personal officer who sat outside the room watching my every move. Again. She wasn't mean like that last time. In fact, she didn't say or do anything.

I didn't know what they thought I could do, being that my hands were tied to the bed for the safety of the hospital staff and myself. Again.

Following X-rays to ensure there were no fractured bones to accompany the bruising to my face from being slammed to the ground, some blood work, and bandages, I was escorted to the police station.

Entry 30

Dear Diary:

Once I was escorted to the interrogation room, the cuffs came off. Finally free, I massaged my wrists. They were sore and somewhat raw. Within hours, I went from tight cuffs to even tighter bed restraints and back to tight cuffs.

The door locking from the other side was a familiar sound. I had watched enough of *The First 48* to know what was about to happen next. I'd sit in the bright, cold room while being studied from recording devices in a nearby area. This would buy detectives time to develop a strategy for approaching me and getting me to confess. There were so many things my body language would reveal. I knew that I would automatically be considered guilty if I went to sleep while I waited. I think they refer to it as "guilty sleep."

I inserted my arms into my short-sleeve shirt to generate warmth as I pondered how I thought this interview would go. I wished they'd hurry up so we could get this over with.

My butt was sore from sitting on the hard, wooden chair that didn't come close to matching the desk. The tingling shifted from my legs to my feet and to my fingertips. Sometimes all at the same time. The bottom of the chair screeched across the cheap linoleum floors when I scooted back to create enough space to lean forward and lay my head against the desk. I guessed they'd accuse me of that "guilty sleep" after all because I was tired and bored from sitting.

Only one officer entered. A female. She held a small notepad and introduced herself by her last name only. Something like Jackson or Johnson. I didn't care to remember. She was unfriendly and smug, and instead of making small talk, she jumped right into questioning me. "What happened to Mr. Sanders?"

I allowed that one question from her. The exhaustion from waiting all that time left me in no mood to cooperate. So I exercised my right to remain silent. I knew that anything I said would be held against me, and since I was no attorney, I was not speaking. "I would like a lawyer."

Officer J. was pissed. The strong ripples that rocked the cedar desk from her fist slamming against it startled me. The smug look on her face when she had first entered turned angry. If I could have read her thoughts, I bet I would have heard her call me a bunch of not-so-nice names.

"You are being booked for murder." That smirk was back. I think she got a thrill out of telling me that since I wouldn't talk to her.

I slept peacefully the first night. Probably because I stayed over in a holding cell. Not much went on there. Pretty quiet and tolerable. There were occasional screams and other mild interruptions like the bars slamming. My body was sore from the hard bench, but I survived. I knew it was a temporary arrangement. Even though I passed on the phone call that was offered to me, I believed Uncle Bobby and Clara would somehow show up to get me, or the jail would realize their error and transfer me to an institution, where my aunt and uncle would be right there for me. Either way, I was going home.

"Sanders."

I jumped up with a smile. *I'm out of here.*

"Put your arms through the bars," the guard instructed.

I was confused. "If I'm going home, why are you cuffing me?"

The officer chuckled. "Your lawyer is here."

"Oh," I said, satisfied. I had no problem with my lawyer taking me home.

He escorted me to a small, gloomy, dimly lit conference room and stood guard just outside the door.

"You're my lawyer?" I asked, taking in the young brunette woman who looked like she had barely graduated high school. She was petite and timid looking.

She extended her hand. "I'm Sarah Harrison your public defender."

"How long have you been a lawyer?"

"Eight years," she said and opened a file. "Myles Sanders is your husband, right?"

"He was."

"Was?" she asked, lacking understanding.

"Yes, was, as in used to be," I said.

"So the two of you were divorced when he died?"

"No."

"Well, why did you use the term 'was' as if you two were no longer together?"

The interview had just started, and I was over these dumb questions already. "Because he's dead which makes him no longer my husband."

She scribbled everything I said on her notepad and asked more and more questions. "Can you tell me what happened to your husband?"

These questions were ridiculous. "Assuming we are stating the obvious, he died," I said.

Sarah laid her pencil down and propped her elbows onto the white folding table that served as our conference table. "Do you think this is some kind of game?" she asked. "You are facing a murder charge. If you didn't need my help, I wouldn't be here. The only way I can help you is if you are honest with me and tell me everything that happened."

Maybe because I'd been taking my medication as directed, everyone had a hard time understanding that I was mentally ill. "People like me don't go to jail. We go to the hospital."

She sat back in her chair and asked, "What do you mean by people like you?"

Since she was my lawyer and her job was to defend me, I had to be honest and tell her everything. "I have been in and out of mental institutions. I am not well up here." I tapped my head. "Ask my aunt and uncle, ask my psychiatrist. His name is Dr. Monroe. He will tell you."

That pencil of hers moved like it was a typewriter. Sarah returned to scribbling everything I said. "What's the institution's name? I want to order medical records to present to the court."

I shook my head. "I disagree with that," I told her. "I have been judged all my life by my family. I don't want the whole world knowing."

"The whole world already knows that you were arrested for murder. It's on the news."

"What? You're joking, right? That's a violation of my rights." I had no clue if what I said was true. *If I am mentally ill, I should be protected.*

"Mrs. Sanders, this is not a joke. I need you to be transparent. What happened to your husband the night he died?"

I cooperated and took Sarah on a trip back down memory lane, only because I needed to miraculously change the narrative of what people thought about me now that my mug was plastered across the TV.

I inhaled, started with the Christmas party at Myles's office, and finished with the night he took his last breath.

"The district attorney will probably offer you a plea deal. It's probably best you take it."

"What does that mean?"

"It means your chance of entering an insanity plea doesn't look good. From what you explained you were in your right mind when your husband died. Taking a plea will ensure you don't get the death penalty."

She didn't provide me with her action plan to get me out of this mess outside of the plea deal that I wasn't going to take.

She didn't even have a plan during court. I didn't even think she knew where to begin.

"No objection, Ms. Harrison?" the judge often asked. It was like he tried coaching her, but she never caught on.

Eight years of practicing law, my ass. It was almost like my case was the first case she had ever tried. She seemed caught off guard. She stuttered and stammered. A kindergartner could have caught on to her uselessness.

Proof of my medical history was submitted to the courts. Instead of Ms. Harrison arguing that I was incompetent to stand trial or face charges for Myles's death, she casually suggested, "There may be a possibility Mrs. Sanders was not in her right mind at the time of her husband's death." I was the one who put that bug in her ear.

I spent a lot of time sighing and drawing stick figures on paper. Ms. Harrison should've sat down and drawn stick figures too, because she was embarrassing us.

When the prosecutor quickly shot that idea down, my so-called attorney didn't have a rebuttal. She instead thumbed through papers that fell out of the manila folder she carried instead of a briefcase.

To put all questions aside regarding my mental state, the judge, not my attorney, said, "The court would like to have Mrs. Sanders undergo a competency evaluation."

"Thank you, Judge," I said out of turn.

He smacked his gavel and reminded me that I was not allowed to speak. I knew that, but I wanted him to understand how much I appreciated his efforts, because my attorney was dumb.

The main question to be answered was whether I could stand trial for the charges against me. Turned out I was. The assessment was quick, painless, and returned unfavorably. Whatever way the chips fell, the outcome would have been the same but at a later date. At least it would have bought me some time. If it were decided that I did not understand the charges brought against me or the nature of the crime, I would have gone through the competency restoration process. After successful treatment, I would have been prosecuted anyway. Something that Ms. Harrison could have gotten me out of if she knew how to do her job.

The question shouldn't have been if I was competent to stand trial but if she was competent enough to represent me. I didn't think she was, especially since she frequently mixed up her cases. She often referred to me as Ms. Parker, and once she called me Myles. It wasn't until I stopped her and reminded her of who I was and what I was dealing with that she regrouped. As we got further into the trial, she proved my theory.

I was called to take the stand, and even I knew that wasn't a good idea. However, Ms. Harrison insisted that I tell them the same thing I told her, and it would help the jury see that I wasn't well. At this point, I wasn't. Mental health treatment in jail was practically nonexistent. Pills, maybe, but don't think about getting an injection.

When I took the stand, the prosecutors trapped me while Ms. Harrison stood by and did nothing.

The prosecutor stood and buttoned his suit jacket. "Mrs. Sanders, please tell the court what happened the night Myles Sanders died."

I leaned into the mic. "We were arguing over me being pregnant."

"So you're pregnant?"

"No."

"Did you lose the baby?"

"I was never pregnant. I only told him that because he was threatening to leave me."

"So you decided to kill him that night because you were afraid he was going to leave you once he found out that you weren't pregnant?"

"I didn't kill him. It was Michael." I had significant loyalty to my brother, but he planted the murder seed in my head, and I figured they'd let me go and pursue him instead. They'd never find him, so the way I looked at it, we would both live freely.

The prosecutor paused. "Who is Michael?"

"My brother."

"Did your brother help you to kill Myles?"

"It was his idea, sir."

"Where is your brother now?"

When I shrugged, the judge reminded me that all answers had to be audible. "I don't know." Anytime I answered a question, I'd look over at the jurors to see if I could gauge their reactions.

The older male prosecutor walked comfortably around the courtroom, sometimes looking at me and sometimes looking at the jurors. He seemed experienced, and his questions never stopped.

"You don't know?" he repeated my answer. "When is the last time you spoke with him?"

"I don't know." That was the truth. "I haven't heard from Michael in a while."

"Estimate. A while like two weeks, months, years?" he pressed.

I thought for a minute. "Sometime after my wedding. Maybe later."

And again, the questions continued without a peep from Ms. Harrison. "How did the two of you usually communicate? Was it email, text messages, phone calls, or all of the above?"

"None of the above, actually. He would talk to me in my ear."

"What do you mean?"

"Just what I said. He spoke to me through my ear whenever he needed to say something."

"What exactly did Michael tell you to do to Myles?"

"He never gave me the whole plan. One task at a time."

He paused again, this time longer than usual. He went over to the desk, looked at a sheet of paper, then held it up to the jurors. It was a picture of my brother. "If you hadn't spoken to Michael since your wedding, how could he have told you to do anything to Mr. Sanders?" He delivered the final blow without an objection from my side.

"I know how it seems, but I can explain," I pleaded from the stand once I realized I was screwed.

"So let me understand fully. The night Myles died, Michael didn't tell you or command you. You just did it?" He raised his voice and asked, "So how do we know that you aren't lying about Michael, who is dead, by the way, the same way you lied to Myles about being pregnant?"

Gasps filled the courtroom. Mrs. Sanders squealed, "God, help me."

"Order." The judge banged his gavel.

I realized then how it sounded. It was too late to change my statement. "Objection!" That came from me, not Ms. Harrison, and wasn't allowed.

"We are going to take a recess. Ms. Harrison, I suggest you get in the mood to defend your client."

Ms. Harrison didn't know how to recover. During the recess, she was even more lost and flabbergasted. She sat across from me with flushed skin while an officer looked on. "We already know that you committed the crime. You should go ahead and plead guilty for reduced charges."

I wanted to take my Sixth Amendment right and represent myself, but the judge was not trying to hear it. My counsel was ineffective. I didn't have Johnnie Cochran money lying around. I couldn't fight for my own life. I had to sit back while Ms. Harrison used me as an experiment in her quest for experience.

She should've focused solely on a mental health argument. She could've presented case studies showing offenders who were not in their right mind when they committed their crimes and how beneficial rehabilitation is versus prison.

The prosecutor was well ahead of her. "Mrs. Sanders's hallucination claims would've been believable, however"—he referred to another sheet of paper—"her blood work on the night of the murder shows consistent medication levels. She was fully aware of what she was doing. Mrs. Sanders became fearful that her husband would leave her, so she announced a fake pregnancy. When Mr. Sanders demanded proof, instead of admitting to her dishonesty, Mrs. Sanders killed him to cover her tracks."

The elder Mrs. Sanders wailed again.

Even as they used my results against me, Ms. Harrison said nothing. I think she had pegged me as a monster the moment she met me. She wanted me to rot.

Not only was my blood work used against me but also my diary. Those entries destroyed any chance of freedom I possibly had. Anytime I had an urge to do something to Myles, I wrote it down. In graphic detail. They read a few passages in court.

"Mrs. Sanders wrote this short entry on the Halloween before Myles died," the prosecutor said and read my words.

Ugh! I hate Myles. It's Halloween, and I'm feeling a little Michael Myers-ish. I wonder if I suggest that we dress up and go trick-or-treating, what he'd say. I'll stuff a knife under my nun uniform, stab him to death, play the victim, and claim someone in a clown costume did it. Who wouldn't believe a nun?

"And then we have this entry," he added and read the detailed account of how I intended to push Myles off the dock at the lake the night we got married.

The prosecutor worked the room delivering his closing argument. "Ladies and gentlemen of the jury. It's simple. Ask yourself this question: if the defendant was taking her medication faithfully as her blood work showed, how could she not have been in her right mind? If the defendant hadn't heard from her brother since around the time she got married, how could he have been responsible for Mr. Sanders's death? Plus, Michael died when he was eighteen years old. As you deliberate, remember the words in her diary."

I watched the twelve jurors, who would then watch the judge read aloud the guilty verdict on all charges including premeditated murder.

Entry 31

Dear Diary:

Getting a visitor in prison was like hearing the ice cream truck coming up the street. As kids we basically had to beg for money. It was the same way in prison. Inmates begged for visitors, letters, commissary. Not me. Not after I had let Mr. Porter talk me into allowing Mrs. Sanders to come for a visit.

She and I made eye contact. The scowl she wore on her face could have torched the entire prison. I slowly shuffled in her direction, regretting the decision to meet with her.

Her voice was cold and low. "Why did you have to kill him?" Heavy tears smeared her mascara.

I was ashamed, embarrassed, and also at a loss for words. I wanted to speak, but no matter what I said, it wouldn't bring any comfort to anyone I had hurt.

"I want details, dammit!" She pounded the table with the side of her fist.

I jumped, startled by her reaction. I'd never seen that side of her, but she had every right to react that way. Pain represented her, and I was the reason why.

"Mrs. Sanders . . ." I shook my head, not knowing what else to say. Court offered plenty of gruesome details.

"So you can kill him and live in the same house with his corpse, but you can't look me in my eyes and tell me why you took my son from me?" She began to sob as her cries echoed throughout the tiny room. When she gathered herself, she said, "My intuition told me you weren't the right wife for him. I told him that numerous times. I begged Myles to divorce you. Had he listened to me, he would still be alive today."

She was right.

"All my son did was love you. He tried to save you from yourself, and look where it got him. Six feet under. You should be dead, not him," she screamed.

Again, she was right.

Because the conversation had gotten heated, the guards ended the meeting.

"I hope you rot in hell," she shouted as I was being escorted out of the room.

After that visit, I never really wanted to encounter anyone from my past ever again. I was content imagining their shame and disappointment without having to see it or hear it.

Needless to say, I was surprised when the guards came to get me for a visit. Because I never completed paperwork for visitors, and Tuesday had already passed, I was eager to see who it was.

"Mr. Porter. We already had our visit. What are you doing here?" I asked, shocked to see him waiting for me in our normal meeting spot.

He wiggled his eyebrows. "Two times in one week."

That was rare. Even more rare was that he showed up with a deck of playing cards. "Gin rummy?" His mood seemed somber.

"Sure." I hid my excitement. I was a skilled gin rummy player. When my mother had free time, she'd always play a couple of hands with Michael and me. Little did Mr. Porter know I was about to spank him the same way I spanked my mother and brother.

"We don't have to draw cards. You deal first," he offered.

I shuffled, allowed Mr. Porter to cut, and dealt myself a dynamite hand. "You okay, Mr. Porter? You seem sad."

He sighed, not offering words.

"Is it your hand? Or the fact that you know you're about to lose?" It felt good to talk trash over a card game.

"I have some news to share with you," he said and pulled a card from the deck and threw one into the discard pile.

I pulled one myself. "Spill it."

I'd won the hand before he spoke again. "Your aunt reached out to me."

I smiled, knowing that he had stayed in contact with Clara. I hadn't. I couldn't. I didn't want to see the hurt and disappointment on her face. Uncle Bobby either. They still found a way to check in on me through Mr. Porter. He'd often send messages from them, always encouraging me, or making sure I knew I was missed. I never sent any back. I honestly wanted them to forget about me and move on with their lives. Happily. I often wondered how much backlash they faced once I was arrested. How much junk Aunt Nora, her friend, and Uncle Buster talked about me to them. I wondered how many times "I told you so" rolled off their tongues. I even wondered if the media camped out in front of their house, trying to score an exclusive interview with the people who raised a killer. I wondered if it forced them to move or go into hiding. I never had the heart to ask. I wanted to forget about them like I wanted them to forget about me.

"Is that right?" I finally said and laid a spread down during our second round.

"I hate to be the one to tell you this—"

"So don't," I rudely told Mr. Porter. I didn't mean for it to come out that way, but I felt like whatever he was about to say would be something painful. I didn't need to hear it. "It's your go."

Mr. Porter placed all ten of his cards face down on the table and sighed again. "Your uncle had a heart attack, and unfortunately, he didn't make it."

I studied and shifted my cards, thinking of what I needed to go out on Mr. Porter.

"Did you hear me, Eva? Your uncle passed away this morning."

"Who, Uncle Buster?" I asked. "It was only a matter of time. His diet was horrible. And the way he and Aunt Nora smoked, I can't say I'm surprised."

"Not Buster, Eva—"

I cut him off before he could say it. "You're losing. Stop stalling." If he didn't say it, it didn't happen.

"Your uncle Bobby passed away this morning, Eva."

He just had to say it. I swallowed the lump of pain and said, "It's your go, Mr. Porter."

He wouldn't play. I collected his cards and started on a game of solitaire. I lost and wasn't in the mood to try again.

We sat in silence as the thoughts of Uncle Bobby no longer rocking in his rocking chair or being a devoted husband and father to Clara and the twins started to register. My leg bounced underneath the table thinking of who'd console Clara like she'd done for everyone else in their times of need. As long as I'd known her, I'd never met any of her

family. The rumors ran rampant about the reason
why. I was just a kid who had unfortunately heard
information that I shouldn't have been privy to
Per usual. Rumor had it, her parents weren't fans
of Uncle Bobby because he dropped out of high
school and worked as a janitor. Clara's parents
refused to pay for the wedding, so they eloped
When her family found out they went through with
the marriage, they disowned her. Maybe it was
true and maybe it wasn't. Either way, I wished I
could be there for her.

"Did I kill him too?"

Mr. Porter shook his head and repeated Uncle
Bobby's cause of death. "Why would you say that?
He died of a heart attack."

I nodded. "Did I cause it? You can be honest, Mr
Porter."

"No one causes a heart attack, Eva. Those things
just happen."

"If that were true, then why do people always say
things like 'You almost gave me a heart attack'?"

"It's just an expression."

I hadn't doubted anything Mr. Porter told me
in a while. In that moment, I did. "You sure about
that? Stress causes heart attacks, and I am certain
that my actions added stress to Uncle Bobby's
heart."

"You can't take the blame for that," Mr. Porter
tried to assure me.

"What will Clara do? They've been together forever. She won't be able to live without him. And then the twins . . ." I paused, thinking of how it felt to lose both parents at a young age. "They are doomed."

"Clara is a strong lady who raised strong kids. They will be fine," Mr. Porter said.

Reality had finally hit me. "No!" I screamed and flipped the table. Cards rained everywhere. One bounced off Mr. Porter's bald head and sashayed to the floor.

The guards rushed in and tackled me.

I could hear Mr. Porter get worked up. "Don't hurt her. Let her go. That's not directed toward me."

It didn't matter what he said. They manhandled me and carried me out of the room, not giving a care about why I had reacted the way that I did. Why would they? I was a mental health inmate. No one cared about us.

Entry 32

Dear Diary:

The day before I was to die by lethal injection, I did something I'd never done since being on death row. I connected with another inmate. Not sexually, but through a conversation that taught me that no matter how you're raised, or what values are instilled in you, anything could happen.

"Hey, inmate in cell six," she called out to me as she had done many times. I just never said anything before. I still planned to remain quiet, but then she said, "I hear tomorrow is your last day. Is that true?"

For us to be confined to our cells twenty-three hours a day, I was surprised she knew that. "It's true, but how do you know that information?"

"Oh, she speaks," she joked. "I used to think you were deaf."

I laughed a little. "Nah, just a loner."

"What's your name?" she asked.

"317—"

"No, silly. Not your prison name. Your real name."

"Oh, sorry. Eva. Eva San . . . Eva Moss," I corrected myself. I didn't deserve the Sanders name.

"Nice to finally meet you. I'm Sandra Baker."

I threw my hand over my mouth to hide my gasps. I wasn't sure what to say next. All that time I had been living next door to *the* Sandra Baker.

"You got quiet on me, number six. Something got your tongue?" She hysterically laughed and deeply coughed like she had smoked two packs of cigarettes a day since popping out of her mother's womb.

I was quiet because I wasn't sure what to say back. That joke was inappropriate coming from her. But the shock of finding out I had lived next to the world's most notorious, most brazen female killer was mind-boggling.

"You still there?" she asked and immediately answered herself. "Of course you're still there. Can't escape this fucker if you tried. Trust me, I've tried." Sandra laughed some more.

It was refreshing to hear. If monsters like her still found a reason to laugh in life, monsters like me could too. When compared to Sandra, what I did to Myles was actually the equivalent of robbing a bank with no customers or tellers. When I think of it, killing Myles was like stealing an ATM compared to her crimes.

"*The* Sandra Baker?" I asked, still in shock.

"*The* Sandra Baker," she repeated. "So you know who I am? Are you scared?"

"No, not at all." Even if I were, there was nothing she could do to me.

"Good. I hate when people are afraid of me. I'm not a bad person. I just did a bad thing. Well, several bad things."

If she wanted to downplay her activities as just "bad," then so be it.

"Are you nervous about tomorrow?" she asked.

I answered, "No," when I realized she couldn't see me shaking my head.

"Good for you. Even if you were scared, don't let them bastards see it. I plan to go out heartless like everyone painted me."

Sandra laughed at the couple of random screams that scared me and briefly halted our conversation. I'd grown used to it, but sometimes it got the best of me.

"I can't wait until it's my turn. Death will be a lot better than here. Hell, if they gave me the option to die by electric chair right now, I'd take it. I'm not afraid of a little shock, you know? I've been shocked before and struck by lightning. So that chair is nothing."

I smacked my teeth at her exaggeration.

"Seriously," she said and tried to convince me. "I was in the pool during a storm, and my parents told me to get out, but I was a hardhead and that lightning got me right here."

I chuckled a bit. "I can't see that, Sandra, and people don't survive lightning strikes."

"They do. I have the burn to prove it."

Truthfully, Sandra was a little scary, yet very intriguing. At least talking to her took my mind off knowing I would die soon. Most people's death came as a surprise. Knowing is different. Knowing is hard and uncomfortable. "I'm going out via cocktail," I offered.

"Yeah, that's how they do it. Painless," Sandra said. "I wonder why they do it that way. Why not give death row inmates the most painful method? Allow them to suffer like their victims and victims' families?"

The back of my head rested against the wall as I thought about how hurt Mrs. Sanders was in court. Sheila too. Mr. Sanders remained emotionless. Perhaps he did that for his family. My mother even popped in my head. I could hear her screams from the night Michael died as if it happened in real time. I imagined Clara's reaction when she learned of Uncle Bobby's death. I still hadn't talked to her. Not once did I offer condolences or call to check on her. I wouldn't have known what to say.

"Do you regret your crimes?" I asked Sandra, thinking about the regret I had for mine.

"None whatsoever," Sandra swiftly replied. "I look at myself as a hero for what I did."

"I remember you from the news," I admitted.

"Yeah, the media covered me like I was a daily thirty-minute sitcom."

That time I laughed. "You're funny," I told her.

"Got to find a way to keep going in here. Just because it's not the life everyone else wanted for me or one that I imagined for myself, it's still life."

"True." Although I had read about Sandra, there was nothing like hearing it from the person herself. There was no telling what people on the outside thought of me or whose version of the story they chose to believe. "What made you kill?" I blurted out but then realized how rude that was. "Sorry, you don't have to answer that."

Sandra chuckled. "It's okay. I've already stood trial. Another won't hurt. Plus, 'killer' will always be associated with my name. I expect people to ask. Never apologize for trying to learn more, no matter what the topic is. Just make sure you're willing to be open-minded enough to change your perception of what you thought the truth was. Got it, cell six?"

I'd lost the respect of my name, and I just wanted that one more time. "It's Eva," I reminded her.

"Eva," she repeated. "Well, *Eva*, I killed because I had to. It was me or them, and I chose me. I hadn't chosen me in a while, but I did that night. However, sitting on death row, I'm pretty much dead anyway, right?"

"Agreed."

"I just choose to make the best of the situation, you know?"

I didn't know, but I agreed anyway. "Yep."

"You know who I am, so you know the story. What most people refuse to believe is all four of those guys had planned to tie me up and rape me. None of that mattered because I was a drug addict who occasionally traded sex for drugs. Everyone had already made their minds up about me. I was trash. You can't be trash and a victim at the same time."

That hit home. Labeling. It was one or the other until the shoe fit.

"I was raped before, you know?"

"I'm sorry, Sandra. I didn't know that."

"Not many people do. So when those men lured me to that warehouse, pulled out that rope, and tried to tie me to that chair, all I saw was a flashback of my camp counselor on top of me, and I did what I had to do. One thing I didn't do was walk the streets without being prepared. Those bastards didn't know, but they found out real soon when I shot them point blank in the forehead."

I instantly felt bad because I had subconsciously done to Sandra what everyone had done to me—attached labels without knowing all the components.

"What about the tongue thing? Why cut their tongues out and leave them on the front porch of their houses?"

Sandra laughed. "Are you sure you aren't some kind of undercover reporter?"

"Not at all. Just curious."

"Honestly, it's because they called me a whore. All four of them were married, and the wives needed to know. I had four free tongues and, well . . ."

"How did you know where they lived?" I asked.

"I went through their wallets, took all the cash I earned for the night, and used their IDs to reunite their tongues with the right house. I still wonder if I mixed them up, though."

In that moment, my original thoughts of Sandra had changed. She was a victim but had been pegged as a monster. Sadly, I kind of wished that during all the times the inmates yelled back and forth through their doors, I had done that too. At least then I wouldn't have always felt so alone six days out of the week and the hours after my visits with Mr. Porter.

"Do you have any regrets with what you did?" Sandra asked.

I nodded. "A ton."

"Like?" she pried. Talking to her was like talking to Mr. Porter.

"Obviously for cutting a life short, but also for the pain I caused to others. Mainly, for not accepting the fact that it was okay to need help. I regret not fighting more for myself."

"It's not too late to have your attorney file an emergency stay of execution, Eva. Life doesn't go easy on a person just because a doctor raised them. Life doesn't go easy on a person just because a scientist raised them. Life isn't necessarily hard on a person just because they were raised by a cashier or a high school dropout. Life is life and filled with various journeys. If you regret not fighting for better, now is the time," Sandra preached.

I shook my head. "I deserve this. Those I hurt deserve this."

"Well, see you on the other side," Sandra said.

"See you."

Entry 33

Dear Diary:

My last entry and final day on earth. For my last meal, I chose none other than Artino's Bakery and Deli. Mr. Porter sat and ate with me. He brought a radio for us to listen to Mrs. Sanders and Sheila's radio interview.

Following the death of Myles, Mrs. Sanders had become a mental health advocate. She was being interviewed, and I was granted the opportunity to listen.

Mr. Porter glanced at his watch. "It's almost showtime. How do you feel?"

I shrugged. "I know that I am about to die. Nothing to feel. I'm not scared if that's what you're asking."

"I'm proud of you, Eva. Although I hoped you would fight your death sentence, sharing your experience will produce great change," Mr. Porter told me.

He had encouraged me to turn over my book of journal entries to spread the word about mental health in the African American community. I finally agreed. Mrs. Sanders reluctantly agreed to publish them as long as the proceeds were donated to mental health facilities across Georgia. I had finally given the book to Mr. Porter. He took it, made copies to submit what had been completed, and returned it to me to continue documenting.

"You just want the whole world to know I'm crazy, huh?" I joked.

"You're not that same person anymore. Your voice will save a lot of people. What you've written in this journal can benefit another person or family living with a mental health illness. That's what I want to show the world. It is possible to get a handle on this illness as long as they act fast and be consistent. Every day won't be good, but with a support system and resources, there can be more good days than bad. You've been on death row for many years, and I have followed your progress. You progressed. Not to mention, you will always make history as one of the few death row inmates to wave all appeals and request an expedited death."

"I'm just glad that I won't be around to face the people's court. The judgment. That was always the worst part. I never understood it. People are not judged for having cancer because it isn't a choice, so why was I being judged for what I have going on, especially since it wasn't a choice?"

"Only one way to get the word out and teach a dual lesson on mental illness and judging," Mr. Porter said. "You've been consistent on your stronger doses of medication and doing well, right? No Michael, no episodes, nothing?"

I chose not to respond verbally. Just a smile. I never told him about the visit from my mother. Nor did I include it in my journal when it first happened. Granted, it occurred before the increase in milligrams, and it was only one time. Hard to feel or think anything when you're a zombie.

I'd never forget hearing my mother's voice. It was shortly after I was transferred to death row. I was totally off my meds, shot and all. Prison didn't care. I think they pretended to keep us safe, but in reality, they hoped we'd go crazy and kill each other. With everything out of my system, all kinds of voices invaded my mind. I didn't recognize any of them, but I knew they weren't Michael. They were loud, strong monsters, and the more I tried to ignore them, the louder they became. Eventually, I got used to them and started talking back. Whispers from me, so no one would hear. Sometimes they were funny, and sometimes they'd tell me to do inappropriate things. At times, I thought about appeasing them because they were my only friends, and I enjoyed the company. I didn't want to lose them, but I also didn't want to do anything to harm anyone or myself.

"My sweet Eva."

"Mom, is that you?" I asked.

"Yes, baby."

"Oh, my God. Is Michael with you?"

"He is. Myles too. We want you here with us, sweet girl."

"How? How do I get to where you are?"

"Hang yourself."

"I don't want to hurt myself."

"Hang yourself, sweet girl. I miss you."

"Is there another way?"

"No. Hang yourself. Go on, do it," she laughed. It was frightening. I covered my ears and rocked back and forth, hoping she'd disappear. *"I miss you. Hang yourself."*

"I can't do that."

"Yes, you can. I need you. Please. Come with us." She sobbed, and then her cries slowly faded away.

"Can't there be another way?" I cried with her.

"No!" she yelled.

My eardrums vibrated, causing me to scream. I always tried to keep quiet, hoping the guards would forget about me. They were such perverts. Always inappropriate remarks or finding a way to cop a feel. Because of my scream, one decided to make a move. He must have sensed my break.

"What's the problem, inmate?" He shined his flashlight into my dark cell.

I shielded the light with my hand.

"You need me to come in there?"

I shook my head.

"I think I need to come in there." He fumbled with his keys, unlocked my cell, and helped himself to me.

"Please, don't," I begged and cried.

"Take off your sock and stuff it in your mouth," he instructed. Because I was slow to react, he lightly choked me. "Don't make me tell you again."

"I will report you," I threatened.

"You're an inmate, and a crazy one at that. No one will believe you. Now turn around." He pushed my shoulder, forcing me to turn. His sweat dripped on me, and he moaned. "You're not so hard in the face like these other girls."

He wasn't the only one. It happened a lot when I first arrived. According to them, I was fresh meat, and sampling me was part of the initiation process. And then it was, "You're pretty, so expect to get lucky often."

Most of them didn't have professional boundaries. It almost seemed as if they took the job just for the sex. I never reported their conduct. I never fought back. I just took it and used my socks to stifle any sound that came out of me. I would lie there while they'd grunt, smack my ass, and force me to call them daddy.

The guards came and went, but their behavior remained the same. Always rude. Always inappro-

priate. Even more shameful, I never got anything
out of it. No contraband, money toward my com
missary. I was just free to be violated and for free
I was convinced they came to work, got off, and
then returned home to their wives like they were
innocent, hardworking husbands.

I was glad to get away from the violation. I fel
terrible for Mr. Porter, though. He was sad that i
was my time. He wanted me to fight for myself, bu
there was no point. I deserved everything I had
coming to me, which was why I didn't appeal. Plus
what would life have been like on the outside? I'd
be sleeping on a park bench or in an alley, riding
the bus through the city, daydreaming. Would
my aunt even want me back at her house? I had
proved that I was capable of hurting my husband
so why wouldn't I hurt her? It was just like Aun
Nora said years ago.

"Oh, they're on," Mr. Porter said when he heard
the host.

"Welcome to Talk Radio. It's May, better known
as Mental Health Awareness Month. We are joined
in the studio today by Mrs. Roberta Sanders. Mrs
Sanders is a mental health advocate and the co
author of the upcoming book *Dear Diary*. Sh
has also appeared on several TV and radio show
promoting the importance of mental health aware
ness. As you may recall, her son, Myles Sander
made national headlines when he was killed b

his wife Eva Moss-Sanders some years back. Eva suffered from bipolar disorder with psychotic features but was found guilty of premeditated murder and sentenced to death. First, let me thank you for being here."

"Thank you for allowing me to use your platform to bring awareness to the people," Mrs. Sanders said.

"Mrs. Sanders, let me start by saying you are an amazing woman. It's one thing to have suffered the loss of your son in such a tragic manner, but then you somehow found the strength to do what you are doing here today."

"My son's death is not in vain."

"What gave you the courage to read the details of your son's death and then agree to share it with the world?"

"Eva's prison counselor reached out to me with the idea. He said he had spent a lot of time with her and felt as if she was a lost soul and that her story needed to be heard."

"What was that like, Mrs. Sanders? Some man reaches out to you with an unorthodox idea?"

"At first, I was upset. I felt as if he was trying to make a mockery of the tragedy. It was actually my daughter, Sheila, who convinced me to move forward with it."

"And what did she say?"

"She felt the same as Mr. Porter. That Eva was a lost soul."

"How did you feel when the first half of the journal entries were shared with you?"

"That's a tough question. I felt a lot of ways. I pride myself on being a Christian woman, but I was having a hard time forgiving her. Sometimes I felt like she deserved the death penalty. But as I continued reading what she'd written, I began to see the lost soul."

"What made you decide to move forward with a publishing deal?"

"Eva suffered in silence for the most part, and I can understand why. Once the most intimate things about you are exposed, it's hard to find people who understand. Honestly, if Eva had approached me about her disorder, I am not sure I would've understood. This is why I am doing this so another family does not have to suffer the same tragedy as mine. Or even suffer as her family did. Her aunt is heartbroken. She and Eva's uncle did the very best they could. We keep in touch. One of the things she beats herself up about is not taking the time to be educated on the subject. Many people don't. There are support groups for the families as well. All I can say is my son's death will not be in vain."

"Eva will face lethal injection today. Do you wish she had appealed?"

"Of course I do. She feels this is what she deserves."

"When is the book scheduled to be released?"

"The final entries will be turned over to me sometime this week, and I will go in and write in my thoughts and feelings. After that, a release date will be set from there."

"As I said before, Mrs. Sanders, you are a courageous woman. Let's take a question from a caller. Caller, what's your question?"

That was it. Mr. Porter clicked off the interview.

"I never got the chance to thank you for showing me Michael's obituary. He seemed so real in my head."

"No need to thank me, young lady. I'm just glad you are getting the word out," he said before standing to leave.

I had enough time to update the final entry and hand it over. I decided to close the diary with a message to every person who has battled and will battle their sanity.

Fighters: Mental health illnesses do not make for an easy journey. One day we're on top of the world, and the next day we feel as if we are fighting against the strongest current. No matter how well we swim, or how hard we try to make it to shore, the current is just too strong. We tire out and begin to drown. Just before we take our last breath, we're rescued, only to venture out into the current again.

Sane people do not understand how hearing "you're crazy" or "you have some loose screws" destroys our world and any hope we have to survive it. Having that stigma placed upon us, remembering to take medication, getting shots, attending therapy, and trying to "behave" in public is a lot. Then every judging eye watching our every move and ostracizing us only causes more pressure.

Professionals say, "In order to get better, you have to follow the treatment plan."

We do and it's still an everyday struggle, even when we follow it perfectly. Still, trust your team. Be willing. Process is possible.

I want you all to know that, while this road is not clear of speed bumps or sinkholes, you should continue to utilize every tool and resource available. Depending on where you live, many options won't be available and assessment and treatment waiting lists are long, but hold on and take advantage of what is there, and do it without shame.

I encourage each of you to learn, learn, and learn some more. Learn how to control the illness instead of it controlling you. Learn about the WRAP plan, which stands for wellness, recovery, action, and plan.

Then *teach* your loved ones how to cope and support you. There are several online resources available and family support groups. They have to be willing.

Ultimately, it's up to you to take charge of your mental health, even without the support of your loved ones. You are your best advocate. Again, I encourage you all to do it without shame. It's okay to speak up and demand to be heard. If your meds aren't working, demand action. If your appetite or sleep patterns are off, speak up. If you're hearing voices, say something, especially if they've gotten aggressive and violent. What you hear is a trick. They are not real. Do not act out anything they are requesting of you.

Be mindful of changes to your body. Sometimes the medication regime takes some adjusting. Think of it as trying on shoes until you find that perfect pair. Some medications come with uncomfortable side effects. Say something.

Please listen to me so you don't have to learn the hard way like I did. It's okay to admit something isn't right. It's okay to accept help. It wasn't until it was too late that I started to take my diagnosis seriously. I had to kill my husband before I took charge of my life. I had to hurt my loved ones, his loved ones, and taxpayers before I realized I should have cancelled out all the naysayers and done what I had to do. I should have spoken up no matter how many times it took.

Hopefully, state legislators and judicial and prison boards will look at my case and take more proactive measures to push for better training for police officers, prison guards, and anyone in the community willing to learn how to effectively engage with the mental health population. Correctional officers need it desperately. There are a high percentage of inmates who are mentally ill. Effective training is critical. The system overall needs to change.

It took a while, but I admit that I committed an awful crime and can't blame anyone but myself. I take responsibility for it all. And therefore, I deserve my fate. My outcome does not have to be your outcome.

To my husband, Myles Sanders, I am sorry.

So long. The guards are here.